Like most seventeen-year-olds, Piper Dunn wants to blend in with the crowd. Having a blowhole is a definite handicap. A product of a lab-engineered mother with dolphin DNA, Piper spends her school days hiding her brilliant ocean-colored eyes and sea siren voice behind baggy clothing and ugly glasses. When Tyler, the new boy in school, zeroes in on her, ignoring every other girl vying for his attention, no one, including Piper, understands why...

Then Piper is captured on one of her secret missions rescuing endangered sea creatures and ends up in the same test center where her mother was engineered. There she discovers she isn't the only one of her kind. Joel is someone she doesn't have to hide from, and she finds herself drawn to the dolph-boy who shares her secrets. Talking to him is almost as easy as escaping from the lab. Deciding which boy has captured her heart is another story...

Books by Sandra Cox

Love, Lattes and Mutants

Published by Kensington Publishing Corporation

Love, Lattes and Mutants

Sandra Cox

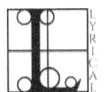

LYRICAL PRESS
Kensington Publishing Corp.
www.kensingtonbooks.com

Lyrical Press books are published by
Kensington Publishing Corp. 119 West 40th Street New York, NY 10018

All Kensington titles, imprints, and distributed lines are available at special
quantity discounts for bulk purchases for sales promotion, premiums, fund-
raising, and educational or institutional use.

Special book excerpts or customized printings can also be created to fit
specific needs. For details, write or phone the office of the Kensington
Special Sales Manager:
Kensington Publishing Corp.
119 West 40th Street
New York, NY 10018
Attn. Special Sales Department. Phone: 1-800-221-2647.

Kensington and the K logo Reg. U.S. Pat. & TM Off.
Lyrical Press and the L logo are trademarks of Kensington Publishing Corp.

First Electronic Edition: February 2015
eISBN-13: 978-1-61650-606-3
eISBN-10: 1-61650-606-7

First Print Edition: February 2015
ISBN-13: 978-1-61650-607-0
ISBN-10: 1-61650-607-5

Printed in the United States of America

For Margaret McNeely

Chapter 1

"Miss Dunn, are we keeping you awake?" Mr. Grumble's sarcastic remark draws titters from the class.

I jerk upright. "No, Mr. Grumble." Heat floods my face.

"Glad to hear it." He turns back to the whiteboard and writes an equation with a red marker.

I slink down in my seat and push my tinted glasses back up on my nose.

The class's attention shifts from my discomfort. Some to the board where Mr. Grumble is still writing the equation, some to flirt outrageously with the new boy in class, some to sneak out their phones and send a text, which most definitely isn't allowed.

Only the new girl—she and the boy are twins—takes time to give me a commiserating smile. I grimace back.

She's always polite and kind in her dealings with me, something that confuses me.

Now her brother, Tyler, although polite, is oblivious. Comes from having girls trip all over him I guess.

The bell rings. I pick up my books. When the room clears, I slide out of my seat. Holly, the new girl, is waiting for me, her entourage grouped around her. She smiles. I glance over my shoulder but the warm smile is for me. She waves her friends on. "I'll catch up."

They move forward like a herd of sheep, perplexed expressions on their faces. Can't blame them, I'm perplexed myself. I don't get a lot of attention. My blonde hair is scraped back into a ponytail and pinned in a wrap-up sponge barrette. My clothes are baggier than a rapper's and as unassuming as I can find. In other words, the total package is boring. I wouldn't go so far as to say that's the way I like it, but it's necessary.

"Hi." Holly shifts her books to her other arm.

"Hi." I clutch my book bag to my chest, not making eye contact.

She falls in step beside me. "Bad luck hitting Grumble's radar. Half the kids in class sleep through his lectures."

I shrug.

"Would you like to grab a latte after school?" is her next conversational gambit.

"Why?" No doubt, I sound like a total jerk, but there's no point in encouraging a friendship. Though the idea of an icy latte and girl talk appeals. A lot. If the situation were different, I'd be a girlie-girl, but it's not and I'm not.

Chatter surrounds us. Juniors and seniors hurry down the hall to their classes. Rosemont is built like a letter U. Freshmen and sophomores on one side, juniors and seniors on the other; the gym and stage merge in the center.

"Because you look like you can use a friend. I know I can."

"I have friends. Everyone has friends." Okay, they're people and creatures I've saved and they don't know who I am, but I'm sure I could count on them in a pinch.

"And a sense of humor." Holly laughs. "Who'd a thought?" She looks me over. Her lips twitch; she tries to hold back a smile.

I grin reluctantly. Then what she tacked on sinks in. "You're the most popular girl in school right now. Why would you possibly need a friend?"

She bites her lips and looks at me.

I cave. "Okay, as a matter of fact, I'd love a latte, but I warn you I'm not noted for my sterling conversation. I'm clueless about the latest trends in hair, clothes, or shoes."

At that moment, her hottie-of-a-brother Tyler lopes by. "Hol," he acknowledges his shorter, fraternal twin. He gives me an absent nod. Not unkind, worse, indifferent. I'm damn sick of fading into the woodwork.

She looks at me as if she's waiting for me to figure it out. I glance from her to her brother. Right. Holly's pretty but hardly drop-dead gorgeous. Though her vivacity makes up for it. And she is the new kid. Still, I get it. The girls are sucking up in the hopes of scoring with her brother.

"Alright, I'll meet you at the Pink Cat Coffee Shop at four o'clock."

She smiles and her pretty features light up. It takes her out of the attractive—but not mega hot—category and puts her in her brother's. "See you at the Pink Cat. Don't stand me up."

"Hey, it's not a date you know." I'm a firm believer in gay rights, but it's so not my thing.

She giggles. "My heart belongs to Ben Henley." She names the football player who was firmly ensconced as the most popular boy at Rosemont until her twin arrived on the scene.

"I'll be there," I promise and head for social studies.

It may not have been smart but having a normal teenage destination to look forward to will certainly make the rest of the day easier to get through. I lied when I said I wasn't interested in hairstyles and shoes. I love girlie stuff. Anyone with a drop of girl DNA loves shoes.

I look at my clothes and sigh. I'll be so glad to get home where I can shuck them like a used cocoon.

For now, I continue the role of uninteresting, blah nerd. I do such a good job even the geeks keep their distance.

With a sigh, I thump my books on my desk and slide into my seat.

For the next forty minutes, I immerse myself in the effects of mob behavior on normal people. As soon as the bell rings, I shoot out of my seat and head for the door.

I hit the hall at a fast pace, not paying as much attention as I should and collide with Edgar the Asshole Fahrenbacher, the most egotistical senior in Rosemont. Although, why anyone with a name like Edgar should be arrogant is beyond me. Maybe he's overcompensating. He calls himself the Stallion. With chestnut hair, tight jeans, and a swagger, he's not bad looking, but his looks don't match his ego.

"Oof." My books go flying and so do his. They hit the floor with a thud.

"Sorry," I mumble, head down, heat shooting through my cheeks.

"Not only are you a mouse, you're a klutz. Pick my books up." Totally humiliated, I bend to comply, hating every minute of it. I would much rather knock him on his swaggering butt and I could do it, too, if I weren't trying to keep a low profile. Well, I could in the water anyway. I can hold my own against anybody in the water.

When I reach for his chemistry book, he kicks it farther down the hall. Embarrassment turns to mad. What a total jerk. Before I totally blow my cover, hands reach out and sweep up the books.

"Which ones are yours?"

I look into piercing blue eyes and forget to breathe—and everything else for that matter.

"Which are yours?" Holly's brother repeats patiently.

Mutely, I point at the top three. He hands them to me before he helps me to my feet. The rest he thrusts at Edgar. "I'm sure you can get the other book yourself," he says easily to Edgar.

Edgar nods, scowling at the interruption of his version of pull-the-wings-off-the-fly.

"Thank you." Breathless, lost in the depths of those deep pools of blue, I forget to disguise my voice. Fortunately—or unfortunately in this case—

it doesn't go with my nerd image. Gramps compares it to mermaids' and sirens' songs. For an old guy, he's a romantic. So when I talk, I try to drop toward an unobtrusive alto.

Tyler's head jerks up. He wasn't paying attention to who he was helping, just being kind to one of the lesser beings. For the first time, he really looks at me and frowns, no doubt trying to equate the voice with the nerd.

I get a firm grip on my books and my raging hormones, and walk hastily away. I can feel his gaze boring into my back, probably trying to see past the shapeless clothes. I shudder, pick up my pace and, of course, trip. I keep a firm grip on my books, right myself, and keep going.

Fahrenbacher's hateful laughter rings in my ears. If only there was a convenient hole to crawl into. My sensitive hearing picks up a murmured, "What a voice."

Tyler's comment echoes in my head as I hurry through wide swinging doors escaping toward sunshine and a blue cloudless sky. I breathe in fresh air, yearning for the scent of salt water.

I turn right amid the cluster of excited voices around me—also anxious to escape the strictures of high school—and head for the coffee shop. It's only a block away. I'll come back later and pick up Beulah, my old truck.

When I arrive at the Pink Cat, Holly has already confiscated a booth. Of course, it's filled by a couple of the more popular girls in school. This is so not a good idea. She smiles and motions me over.

I shake my head and straighten my shoulders. I'll at least get my latte. I wait in line and, when I get to the counter, mumble my order.

Ignoring Holly, I grab my latte and head for the door.

"Piper," Holly's voice rings out. I cringe but take another determined step toward the door.

"Piper," Holly bellows again.

I sigh. So much for anonymity. I turn and prepare for twenty minutes of hell. After that, I'll make my escape. This is such a stupid idea.

I drag my feet over to her table.

"There you are." She beams. "Sit down. Piper's going to help me with my chemistry," she explains to the two cheerleaders sitting with her. They rise with alacrity.

"Uh, catch you later, Hol. Cheerleading practice starts in half an hour," the taller one says.

"Give our best to your brother," the other chimes in.

"Of course," Holly responds sweetly.

They grab their drinks, murmur a hello in my direction, and trot out the door.

"You were going to stand me up," she accuses.

I shrug. "I'm lousy at chemistry."

"I'm pretty good at it," she responds with a mischievous smile.

"You're bad. I like it." As always, except for that one slip with her brother, I use my nerd voice. This girl is way too bright.

She gives a modest smile and sips her cappuccino, loaded with whipped cream and chocolate sprinkles.

She glances disparagingly at my no-frills iced latte. "That looks very plain."

"It fits me." I take a sip and sigh with pleasure as the bite of espresso and the smooth taste of chocolate coalesce and slide down my throat.

She leans forward, her expression both curious and knowing. "Plain's exactly what you're not, but for some reason you want people to think you are."

Startled, I jerk upright. The cup, slick with condensation, starts to slip from my hands. I set it down hastily.

"What are you talking about?" My stomach jumps.

"You're the only girl in school who hasn't tried to befriend me in order to get to my brother. It piqued my curiosity." She places her elbows on the table, rests chin in hands, and studies me.

I squirm. "He's not my type. I've barely noticed him."

"Oh, you've noticed him all right. Even with those tinted glasses, I've seen you follow his progress down the hall. So why haven't you tried to worm your way into my good graces?"

Why indeed? My brain shuts down. "I'm shy," is all I can think of.

"Maybe." She sips her frothy drink and leans back, her gaze still on me.

"Your brother isn't the complete God's gift to women everyone seems to think he is." Liar. Liar.

"That's telling me," an amused voice speaks over my shoulder.

Crap! Busted.

Chapter 2

I'm so going to die of embarrassment. And after he chivalrously came to my rescue when I smashed into Edgar the Asshole.

I straighten my shoulders and mumble in a rough alto, "I'm sorry, that was very rude of me after you helped me earlier." When I first decided to change my voice, I should have gone for high and squeaky. It would have been in keeping with Fahrenbacher's mousy image of me, but it's too hard on the voice box.

"What happened?" Holly's eyes widen and she leans forward.

"I collided with Edgar Fahrenbacher. Your brother came to my rescue before Fahrenbacher could turn me into his boot-licking slave," I say with more asperity than I mean to.

I feel a lean hip press against mine as Tyler lowers himself into the booth. The warm thigh squeezing intimately against mine sends a sharp jolt of electricity through me. It takes every ounce of self-control I possess to keep from leaping over him and running for the door. Instead, I nonchalantly ease over to give him room.

Can he hear the erratic thumpity-thump of my racing heart?

"Fahrenbacher's full of himself but harmless." He acknowledges an acquaintance at another table with a lift of his hand.

"I wonder." I'm good at reading people. I can sense more at an elemental level than most folks bogged down by social mores cluttering their perceptions. Beneath Fahrenbacher's social facade of arrogance is meanness and cruelty. He bears watching.

Before Tyler can respond, three girls from my lit class come over and flirt shamelessly with him.

"Take your entourage and go away, bro." Holly waves him off.

He grins and rises. "See you at home. Bye, Piper."

I nod.

He ambles away, the three girls in his wake.

"Now you've done it." Holly shakes her head and sighs. She throws her voice to be heard above the chatter going on around us.

"Um?" Tyler strides with a loose-legged gait to the counter. I love the way his soft, faded jeans cup his extremely pinchable butt. He and his harem place their order.

I shift and give Holly my attention. "Done what?"

"You've become his latest cause."

My ears tingle. Something's wrong with my hearing. "Excuse me?"

"Tyler's a big believer in accountability. Now that he's come to your rescue, he'll view you as his responsibility."

"I am not his responsibility nor do I desire to be." I jab at the ice in my latte with my straw. Yeah, right. For a moment, I imagine myself as Tyler's responsibility. A second later, sanity returns. "It's entirely unnecessary. I'm equipped to take care of myself." Better than most.

Tyler goes outside. The three girls trail after him. "He seems to have gotten over it." I watch, through the glass wall, as the girls flirt their empty heads off. I immediately feel ashamed. I have no way of knowing whether their heads are empty or not. Mortification surges through me. I'm jealous.

Holly smiles knowingly. "The bro has that effect."

"I don't know what you're talking about." My belly knots. Holly Carlisle sees entirely too much. I suck down the rest of my latte and stand. "Thanks. It's been..." My voice trails off as I try to figure exactly what it has been.

"Educational," she suggests, eyes twinkling.

"You're a witch," I accuse.

"And you mean that in the nicest possible way." Her shoulders shake with suppressed laughter.

The girl is incorrigible. I shake my head and beat a hasty retreat.

"See you tomorrow," she calls.

I wave a hand over my head and keep walking.

He can't have seen me with his back to the door, but before I can push through it, he reaches behind and pulls it open. Startled, I dart through. My head down, I try for inconspicuous.

"See you, Piper."

His awareness of me catches me off guard. I don't know what to make of it. He's the prince and I'm the frog—or dolph-girl. I nod and pick up my pace. The girls smile in a friendly fashion. Maybe, I've misjudged them, never given them a chance.

Again, I have the uncomfortable feeling that his gaze follows me. As soon as I'm out of sight, I pick up my pace.

"Piper, wait." Footsteps sound behind me.

Crap.

Why can't he and Holly leave me alone? I want to shake my hair free, lose the nerdy glasses and clothes, and jump into the ocean, free to be myself. What can he possibly want with me? I've gone out of my way to be invisible and he's surrounded by girls.

"Where are you headed?" He catches up with me easily. I'm five-eight and have long legs. He's six-two and has longer.

I stop, muttering sea curses under my breath. He and his sister so unnerve me.

I hunch into my shapeless shirt. I've had way too much human interaction today. It's giving me a headache, all sorts of uncomfortable feelings surface. I desire peace and the sea to counter the raw and edgy.

I shift toward him. "What do you want, Tyler?" I muster what patience I have left. It's time for me to patrol the waters.

He shoves his hands in his pockets and rocks back on his heels. His expression amused. "You're an intriguing little thing. I've never had this effect on a girl before."

Little thing? Maybe to someone six-two.

No one has ever bothered to look beyond my nerdy surface. Now, in a short period of time, both he and his sister are probing.

I know why Holly is. My lack of interest in her brother fascinates her. And I think I know why Tyler is interested, too. It's my own damn fault. I was careless about my voice and it's come back to bite me.

A light breeze ruffles his thick tawny hair. High cheekbones emphasize chiseled bone structure. My gaze drifts to a very kissable mouth before I jerk it back to those oceanic blue eyes that give me a drowning sensation.

His expression goes from amused to thoughtful. "I was wondering if you'd like to go on my boat Saturday."

"You have a boat?" The boy continues to surprise me.

"Yeah. My mom said if she didn't know better she'd swear she and dad spawned a fish." His eyes crinkle with laughter, inviting me to share in the joke.

Mine narrow. The comment hits too close to home.

"Why?" I fist my hands on my hips. "Why do you want to take me on your boat? Is this some sort of joke or locker room bet?"

He frowns, as if taken aback. Definitely not used to hearing no from females, especially dowdy ones.

Recovering, he drawls, "I have a theory I'm trying to prove."

"Which is?" I narrow my eyes and angle away from him.

"That a girl lurks beneath that getup." He reaches for my glasses.

I slap his fingers hard enough to make him back up and shake his hand.

"Ouch. Why'd you do that?"

"The sun hurts my eyes."

"It's behind a cloud." He points out the obvious.

"You have every other girl in school, isn't that enough?" I storm, panting.

"Apparently not."

Chapter 3

I hurry to my truck with more speed than grace. Big, rusty and ten years old, it doesn't elicit any vehicle lust among the other students. It's a gas-guzzler, but it serves its purpose for trips down the coast. Hunching over the wheel, I mutter as I drive. "It was the voice." Mortification assails me. I've never slipped up since I started the charade four years ago, when I went through puberty. That's when my voice and eye color changed. Who'd have thought dolphin and human DNA would mix to give me the voice of a sea siren? The blowhole on my back I'd been born with. Luckily, from a distance it looks like a birthmark.

Lowering my voice from its normal melodic tone to a deeper alto is second nature to me, or was till I looked into a pair of sea-blue eyes.

Grinding my teeth at my loss of control, I rip off the offending barrette. My hair flies around my shoulders as I shake it free. Tension rips through me. I've spent too much time on land breathing in smog-filled air. I desperately need the soothing waves of the sea, the song of the whales and the swaying, jewel-like glitter of coral on the ocean floor.

I'm on my way home before I remember Gramps mentioning yesterday he was almost out of oatmeal. I do a U-turn, stop at the local grocery store, and then head home again.

Finally. I turn off the paved lane onto a dirt road. At the top is a cliff with the best view in California.

Eight minutes later, I kill the motor and just sit there, my arms resting on the steering wheel.

I toss my glasses on the seat, the better to enjoy the view. They are oversized, pink tinted, and do a good job of hiding my unusual turquoise eyes. The problem is they distort my vision.

Waves lap below. I've gotten home later than usual. Lights across the bay have already begun to glisten like stars. My taut muscles loosen. I will never lose my fascination for the ocean. It's my existence. I can't imagine living anywhere but here.

I take one last look at the isolated outcrop we live on before getting out of the truck and entering the cottage. The aromas of spaghetti and garlic bread waft around me, tickling my senses. My mouth waters.

Gramps stands at the stove in jeans and a plaid shirt, a plain white apron wrapped around his lean middle, stirring a pot.

A wave of love engulfs me. This man is my family. He looks like an aging tree, tall and stooped with a shock of white hair. He worked the coast as a salmon fisherman until the salmon were nearly decimated from overfishing. Now he takes the occasional tourist junket out. With its location, Gramps could sell our cottage and live the rest of his life like a king, but not only does he love it, the location is paramount to me.

I come up behind him and hug his ropy waist. "Sorry I wasn't home to take care of supper." I lay my cheek against his back.

"What, you think I can't cook?" It's a standing joke between us. Cooking isn't either of our fortes but Gramps is far better than I am. He glances at the clock. Five o'clock. Suppertime at the Dunn household. "Sit down and eat before you dart out to save the world."

I know better than to argue, especially the way my stomach is growling. "I'll set the table."

I hum as I put out plain white plates on the little table. The kitchen is homey, all pine and yellow paint, with white curtains at the window. Encompassed in the warmth of the room, I momentarily forget my need for the sea.

Gramps pauses to listen, a look of pleasure on his face. I have no need to disguise my voice here.

I fill our glasses with iced tea. Moments later we eat, my fork loaded with slippery pasta. I break a piece of hot bread apart. Steam, tinged with the aroma of herbs, rises and tickles my nose. I shift and glance up.

Gramps pauses; his gnarled hand circles his iced tea glass. "You look so much like your mother," he says softly.

"Tell me again, how you found her," I urge. I've heard the story a hundred times, but since I've lost her, I never tire of it. She and my dad were killed in a car wreck when I was four. There's some mystery surrounding their death. Dad was speeding and took a curve too fast. Gramps maintains he would have never driven that fast with my mom in the car without a darn good reason.

I miss my parents. It breaks my heart that my memories of them are fading. My clearest recollection is swimming beside my mother, her hair rippling in the water like silk, her body as supple as a seal's, laughing and chattering like an otter.

I shake myself back to the present and focus on Gramps.

A faraway look in his eyes, he leans back in his chair, takes a deep breath, and begins. "Richard and I were out fishing. The night before there'd been a terrible storm. We found her clinging to the side of the boat."

My mind drifts while he tells the story, remembering the parts he's leaving out. That mom was a lab rat. She never knew where the lab was or whom it belonged to: the government or a private investor. She was either stolen or an orphan. They altered her germ line by adding dolphin DNA. The germ line that was passed on to me.

Without thought, I rub the blowhole between my shoulder blades. I focus on Gramps.

"She was fourteen and your dad was seventeen. They looked at each other and that was that. I don't know who fell in love with her first, Richard or your grandma. We raised her like one of our own. The only one who never considered her a family member was your daddy and he married her."

"And they were happy," I prompt, my elbows resting on the table, my chin in my hands.

"I've never seen anyone happier." He rolls pasta on his fork and pops it in his mouth. He chews and swallows before saying softly, "We were all happy."

Poor Gramps. I know he misses Grams and his children. Grams died five years ago. She went to sleep one night and never woke up. I reach over and squeeze his hand. "You still got me, Gramps."

He rolls his hand over and grasps mine. "I sure do. You're the joy of my life. I'm a lucky man." He drops my hand. "Now finish eating and get out there and save the ocean world."

"Why do you think they picked Mom?" I asked around a mouthful of pasta.

He taps his fingers together and looks into the distance. "I don't know. But if I was to guess, I'd say at some point they saw her swim when she was little more than a toddler. Whoever did that to her would have wanted someone with an affinity for the ocean." The faraway look in his eyes disappears and he slaps his palms against the table. "Get going, girl."

I wolf down my food and carry my dirty dishes to the sink.

"Leave them. I'll take care of it."

"Thanks, Gramps." I hurry to my little room at the end of the hall and step out of my offending clothes. Under them, I'm wearing a bright turquoise two-piece. I take a quick look in the mirror. Satisfied, I trot out of my room and down the hall. "Bye." I let myself out the door and jump off the deck into thick blades of grass that tickle my feet.

A few yards behind the house is the edge of the cliff. I wrap my toes around the rocky ledge and push off. The wind pulls at me as I bullet through the air. The water barely splashes when I hit it and go straight down. I pull into a ball, turn in a circle then stretch out my arms and cut through the water. It ripples around me, warm and smooth as a lover's caress. I push to the surface and chuff to blow water out of my crescent-shaped blowhole, before diving back down. My eyes adjust to the clear dark water. My hair floats out around me.

Multi-color coral catches my eye. Entranced, I circle it. Water ripples. I whirl sharply. That's when I see the fins.

Chapter 4

I turn right. A dark fin circles. I turn left and see another, and another. The circle closes around me, coming closer and closer. A gray shadow dives beneath me and shoots toward the surface.

I wrap my arms around the friendly dolphin and giggle in delight, bubbles dotting the water. The other dolphins circle and dive around us. We frolic, playing hide and seek between the glittering coral reefs. A school of bright yellow fish glides by. Startled, they scatter.

We swim around a mile out when the dolphins begin to chatter, making whistling sounds. I listen, then hear it too, a pod of blue whales heading toward the shallows, no doubt following krill.

I have to get the whales turned around before they hit the shoal. I swim toward them. My dolphin friends trail behind. The whales' song becomes stronger. If the situation weren't so dire, I'd enjoy listening to them. This group is happy. When they finally come in sight, I swim back and forth in front of them. Their massive bodies dwarf me. They slow and watch me curiously.

The dolphins chatter, their fins swinging from side to side, swishing cool salty liquid. In response, the lead whale lobs the surface. The wave knocks me up and out of the water. I land with a loud splash.

The dolphins circle me chattering in agitation.

I shake myself and head back toward the whales. The whale that caused the small tsunami noses me in apology. I pat him and swim past, careful of his tail.

The dolphins continue to chatter. The whales respond, roll on their sides, turn around, and swim back toward the ocean.

I blow bubbles out my mouth and manage a credible chatter. The dolphins chirp back at me.

The rest of the night passes uneventfully. Around one-thirty, I remember my English Lit paper. I take one more cruise around the bay then head home.

It takes me two hours to write the darn thing. I proof it and slip into bed. The alarm beeps insistently less than three hours later. "Nooo." I pull the pillow over my head, already drifting back to sleep.

"Honey, it's time to get up. If you don't, you'll be late for school." Gramps raps his knuckles against the door.

"Coming." Resigned, I unbury my head.

His footsteps disappear down the hall.

I stretch like a cat, get up, stumble to my tiny bathroom, and throw water on my face. With short, impatient strokes, I gather my hair back before I throw on my clothes. With great reluctance, I put on my glasses. I grimace in disgust at my appearance. I look more like a mouse than a dolph-girl. Oh well. Even Superman had his mild-mannered, nearly invisible counterpart: Clark Kent.

My mood lightens exponentially as I open the door and smell the seductive scent of pancakes and fresh-brew. Of their own accord, my steps hasten to the kitchen.

"Thanks. This looks wonderful." A stack of pancakes on a plain white plate, orange juice, and a steaming cup of coffee sit on the table. I slide into my chair.

"Eat up." He stands at the stove. Batter pops and hisses as he ladles it into a cast-iron skillet.

My stomach rumbles. Gramps doesn't have to ask me twice. Swimming the sea burns an unbelievable amount of calories. I have the appetite of a football player and never gain an ounce.

I suck down a fluffy hot stack swimming in butter and maple syrup, grab my books, and head for the door.

"Have a good one. Did you get your homework done?" Gramps scoops flapjacks out of the skillet and sits down to eat his breakfast.

"Sure did. You have a good one, too." I blow out the door and hop in my truck. The engine rumbles to life. A white puff of smoke sputters out the tail pipe as I head for school.

I chug into the parking lot and have the satisfaction of seeing Fahrenbacher blanch as I pull alongside his sleek black 350Z, my wheel base inches from his own. He jerks the wheel sharply and the car swerves to the right, almost into another parked car.

He waves his third digit at me.

I bare my teeth and pull my old truck directly in front of him to snag a parking spot. There will be reprisal, but even Clark Kent occasionally forgets his meek disguise.

Bam. I slam the door on my old truck. I have to slam it for the latch to catch.

Fahrenbacher parks his car, jumps out, grabs my shoulder, and yanks. His fingers close around a handful of cotton fleece. I leave my sweatshirt behind and beat a hasty retreat. Luckily, my disguise is intact. He has a hundred pounds on me. I've put off taking self-defense classes because I don't have any extra time. I'll have to rethink that.

I nearly step on the person in front of me getting through the door. I glance over my shoulder. Fahrenbacher glares at me, his face red, hatred in his eyes. He mouths, "You're going down."

"Loser." I mouth back.

He lunges.

I scurry to my class and sit down as the bell rings.

Fahrenbacher sticks his head in the door and starts forward. The English teacher looks up from the roster. "Mr. Fahrenbacher, do you want something?"

He shakes his head, frustration on his face.

"Then I suggest you get to your class."

He stares at me, his face an ugly purple, before he storms out.

I don't realize I sat next to Holly until she leans over and whispers. "What did you do to God's gift to women?" She wears a fitted white cami over an ocher, fitted tee that brings out the highlights in her hair. A light floral fragrance tickles my nose.

"Beat him to a parking spot and nearly scratched his sports car." I speak out of the side of my mouth.

Miss Sweeney looks at me, her eyebrows lift. I open my notebook, pull out a pen, and put my industrious-student-ready-to-soak-up-all-knowledge expression on. Her attention shifts. "Good morning, class."

Since it's first hour, she gets a half-hearted response, along with several barely concealed yawns.

The weight of a stare that isn't Miss Sweeney's causes my head to swivel sharply right. My glance collides with intense blue eyes.

Our gazes lock. Energy crackles. He breaks contact long enough to look at the doorway Fahrenbacher disappeared through before he shifts his attention back to me and raises his eyebrows. The boy doesn't miss much. Neither does his sister for that matter.

I shrug my shoulders.

"Ms. Dunn."

My head swivels toward the teacher.

"What is the oldest known piece of significant literature in the English language?"

I clear my throat. "Beowulf."

She gives me an approving smile. "That's right, Ms. Dunn." She goes into lecture mode and I slouch down in my seat. I can feel Tyler's stare. My skin quivers. It's like a touch. I ignore him—or at least try to—focusing my attention on the instructor. The problem is my reaction to him is more than just physical. I've come to realize Tyler Carlisle is more than just a pretty face. The more I'm around the guy, the more I like him. He's so sweet and funny. I straighten. I'm pretty sure I've been staring at the teacher with a dopey smile plastered on my face.

When the bell rings, my feelings are mixed. I won't have the distraction of Tyler for the next hour.

Holly scoops up her books and waits for me. I rise reluctantly. I like Holly but doing the girlfriend thing is such a bad idea.

Ann Jones, the class president who sits in the row in front of us, turns. "Are you heading for study hall, Holly?"

"I am, but I'm waiting for Piper. I'll catch ya later." She smiles at Ann. Holly has one of those smiles that zeroes in and makes you feel like the most important person in the world, like basking in sunshine.

"Okay." Ann smiles back, looks at me, and smiles politely. I swear she just stopped herself from shaking her head in bewilderment. I feel like commiserating. I certainly can't see what my attraction for the twins is.

Tyler waits at the door. He falls into step as we walk down the hall. Hurried footsteps clatter around us. The scents of books, sweat, and uber-strong aftershave surround us. It's as natural as the smell of coconut in sunscreen.

"Tyler, your class is in the other direction," Holly points out, shifting her books more securely in her arm.

He ignores her and looks at me. "What did you do now to piss Fahrenbacher off?"

"I have no idea what you're talking about," I reply with all the dignity I can muster.

"Come off it, Piper. Fahrenbacher has a hair-trigger temper and he's psychotic. You need to stay out of his way."

It didn't help that I'd been telling myself the same thing. "Maybe he should stay out of mine," I shoot back. "Yesterday you said he was harmless."

"I lied. Sue me. I was trying to make you feel better."

Holly clears her throat. "All right, children, play nice."

"Tyler, you need to get to class. I'll take care of Piper."

He snorts. "Oh yeah, the five-foot blonde, taking care of the five-foot-eight blonde. Don't worry, Mr. Smith likes me." He refers to his history teacher.

"Why are you doing this?" Heat rushes up my chest and pools in my face and neck. I've let my voice slip again.

Her expression curious, Holly glances from one to the other of us before she slides through the door to study hall. At least, my voice doesn't seem to have an effect on her.

"Damned if I know, but I think it's got a lot to do with the voice. I can't help wondering if beneath the camo, the package matches those golden tones." He studies me as if trying to pierce my disguise.

"I have no idea what you're talking about," I respond in hoarse tones before I turn my back on him and hurry into the room. I glance back. He's watching me with an intent expression. When he catches my glance, he winks and saunters off.

Holly motions me toward an empty seat beside her. I sigh and slide in. Life is getting complicated. Other than sea turtles and dolphins, I've never had a friend before. I'm not sure how to act.

I glance at the hall monitor. He's talking to a student at his desk. I lean over and whisper to Holly. "Is your brother always like this?"

"I told you, once he helps someone he feels responsible. Although, he does seem to have taken it to a whole new level with you. If you were more his type I'd say he was interested." She gives me a speculative look. "But you most definitely are not."

I wince.

"Are you?"

She takes me off guard.

"Say what?"

"Underneath those frumpy clothes and ghastly glasses are you Tyler's type?"

"How in hell would I know?" I snap.

"Would you like to go shopping?" She leans forward eagerly. "We could have a girls' night. I could fix your hair and show you how to use make up. It would be fun."

Her whole face lights up. I hate to rain on her parade, but this idea has to be nipped in the bud.

"No way. Take me as I am or don't." That's as clear as I can make it.

"Fine." She thrusts out her lip.

Oh great.

"Ladies, quiet." The hall monitor has finished his conversation and is determined to end ours. Works for me.

Holly ignores me and pulls out her notebook. She begins to write industriously. I glance at her paper that's angled in my direction. This isn't the end of it.

I sigh. I knew this friendship thing was a mistake. I'm not sure which twin is more stubborn. The genes fall pretty evenly between them.

Flipping open my lit book, I ignore Holly and get down to work. I actually have most of my homework done when the bell rings.

The rest of my classes pass faster than I expect. When the bell rings for the last class, I race for my truck. I breathe a sigh of relief when I make it out of the building with no sign of Fahrenbacher.

When I get to my truck, I see why. My tire is slashed.

Chapter 5

"Dammit," Heat courses through me. I could swear my blood is boiling.

"At least he didn't slice all four." Tyler stands behind me, hands on hips, studying my flat tire.

I whip around. "And I should be grateful?" Fuming, I yank open the door of the truck, lean in, and pull the jack out from under the seat.

Tyler moves me out of the way, engages the emergency brake, then takes the jack out of my hands.

"What are you doing?" My jaws are locked so tight I have to push the words out.

"I'm going to change your tire." He squats down, pries off the wheel cover, and unscrews the lug nuts.

"I know how to change a tire."

"No doubt." A nut bounces out of the wheel cover and lands on the ground. I pick it up and toss it back. It clinks, spins, and then settles. I start to get the tire from underneath the truck bed but again am interrupted. Tyler nudges me aside with his hip.

Part of me appreciates the blatant male attitude. I quickly squelch it. "While I appreciate your help, it's completely unnecessary. I can do that." I reach for the tire.

"My father would turn over in his grave if I let a girl change a tire when I'm around." He holds it easily away from me and squats down to slide it onto the axle.

I roll my eyes. "Your father's alive."

"Yeah, so it's important we keep him that way."

I bend down so we're on the same level. "Why are you doing this?"

"I just told you."

"That's not what I mean and you know it."

"Afraid I don't." He turns his attention back to the tire. A motor coughs behind us. White smoke spits from a clunker leaving the lot, followed by a new but dirty compact, a winking girl decal on the bumper sticker.

"Why are you having anything to do with me?" I can't figure it out. "There's not a girl in school who isn't falling all over you." As if to emphasize my point, two sophomores walk by giggling and poking each other, as they stare at Tyler's hindquarters encased in tight soft denim.

"Except for you." He spins on a lug nut. The traffic leaving the parking lot picks up.

"Is that what it's about? The one you can't have?"

"Can't I?"

His voice lowers to a velvet swirl of sound.

"Look at me." I flip my hands from my shoulders to my thighs. "I've seen the girls that chase after you. You don't have to settle."

He sighs. "Haven't we had this conversation before? Besides, you're making too much out of me changing a tire." He turns back to the lug nuts.

Heat floods my face. "Sorry." I stand and slap dust off my pants.

"I'm still planning on taking the boat out Saturday. Have you thought about going with me?" He twirls the last nut on and pushes to his feet.

"No." I fight back regret. "And you shouldn't go either. A storm's coming in."

"The weatherman disagrees. It's supposed to be sunny with a light breeze." He puts the jack away and dusts his hands.

I open my mouth to argue when a shadow falls across my feet. Fahrenbacher stands leering at me. "Keep that heap away from my car. You even smudge it you'll be sorry."

All the bewildered feelings that Tyler's presence brings to the surface coalesce into one hot ball of anger. "You jerk." I ball my fists and lunge.

Tyler grabs my shoulders, pulls me back, and steps in front of me. "You wouldn't know anything about this would you, Edgar?"

"This has nothing to do with you, Carlisle."

"Piper's a friend of mine. I don't like my friends messed with." He straightens, his body language unmistakable. Fahrenbacher's bigger and burlier but something about the way Tyler carries himself makes me think it would be a mistake to tangle with him. I've a feeling Tyler's mild exterior hides raw passion. I hope Fahrenbacher has figured it out, too.

"Friend?" Fahrenbacher raises his eyebrows, his expression disbelieving. "Have you started slumming?"

In a movement too fast to follow, Tyler slams him up against my old truck. It happens so quickly, I barely have time to process what's happening.

"Fight," a pimply-faced freshman sings out. Most of the students are already in their cars or out of the parking lot. The ones left come running.

"Tyler, let him go." I tug at his arm. Taut muscles beneath my hand quiver and jump.

"You owe her an apology."

"She's going to be waiting a long time," Fahrenbacher spits out. "Now let me go before I tear your freaking head off."

The students around us quiet and quickly disperse. It can only mean one thing. I glance around and see Mr. Myers, the basketball coach, striding toward us. "It's Mr. Myers."

Tyler drops his hand and takes a reluctant step back.

Fahrenbacher straightens and pulls away from the truck. He raises his chin and straightens his collar in typical male fashion.

"What's going on here?" Mr. Myers stares at the boys suspiciously. He's tall and rangy, and wears his light brown hair cropped close to his head, his blue striped shirt tucked neatly into khaki pants.

"Just changing Piper's tire." Tyler's easy smile is firmly in place. He squats down, picks up the jack, and slides it under the seat.

"I suggest you all quit loitering in the parking lot. Fahrenbacher." He shifts toward Fahrenbacher, his gaze level.

"Just leaving." His shoulder slams against Tyler as he strides away.

Tyler's eyes spark and his jaw hardens, but only for a second. He calls in a casual voice after Fahrenbacher, "I'll catch you later."

Fahrenbacher stops and looks back, his expression full of menace. "I'm counting on it." He stomps to his car, guns the motor, and drives away. Once out of the parking lot, he squeals the tires and peels out.

"Tyler."

"Yes, Mr. Myers?"

"Whatever issues you've got with Fahrenbacher, keep it off school grounds." He pauses before he adds, "Watch your back."

"Yes, sir."

Mr. Myers turns and trots back toward the school building.

Tyler and I stare at each other.

"You be careful." I pluck at a piece of lint on my pants. Not that it's noticeable in the baggy creases.

"*You* be careful."

Before I realize what he means to do, Tyler reaches out, grabs my shoulders, and gives me a light shake. His touch electrifies.

I stare at him, mute, before common sense returns. I step away and he drops his hands. I wonder if he felt that current of electricity, too. By the way his eyes darken, I suspect he has.

My gaze wanders to his mouth. If such a light touch has this effect, what would those delectable-looking lips be like? My breath catches, appalled at the direction my thoughts take.

He clears his throat. "I can take care of myself. But you are so tiny a good breeze could blow you away."

I lift my chin. "You couldn't possibly know that."

"Those edgy cheekbones don't show on someone buried in fat."

"My glasses hide my face." I touch my cheeks, self-conscious.

"Unless you happen to be looking from the side." He grins.

"Why are you looking at all?" I shoot back.

"Damned if I know. It's certainly not your winning personality and I have no idea about your looks." He grins as he gives me a once over. "You look like you're in disguise."

His grin lights me up inside. I fight off its effect. "It's not a disguise. It's me." It's all I can do not to gag. This? Me? Ha!

"Are you going out on the boat with me tomorrow?" He shifts his weight just as he shifts his conversation, catching me off guard.

"I already told you, no, I'm not. And, I repeat, you shouldn't either."

"If you change your mind, call me." He rattles off his number before he ambles away.

Mentally, I toss up my hands. Why do I bother?

Chapter 6

Sunlight filters through the blinds. I roll out of bed, pad to the window, and draw them up, blinking in the bright light. Raising the window, I sniff the breeze. Beneath dazzling sunlight, I smell the storm. By the pressure in my head, it's going to be a doozy. The doctor blames the pain on sinuses. I know better.

I reach for my cell on the nightstand and call Holly. She gave me her number when we were doing the girlie thing over lattes. The phone goes to voice mail. I glance at the clock. Eight AM. She must still be sleeping. Maybe Tyler changed his mind.

I let the blinds drop. Still dressed in the pink boxer shorts and white French tee I slept in, I head for the kitchen. The rich scent of brewed coffee beans tickles my senses as I wander into the cheery yellow room.

"Hi, Hon." The papers rattle but Gramps doesn't look up. He sits at the pine table, a mug of steaming coffee at his elbow. A coffee ring stains the tablecloth.

I pull out a white cup and bowl, pour myself a cup of coffee, fill the bowl with milk and cereal, and sit down.

Gramps folds his paper and drops it on the table. "You're on your own for dinner. I'm taking a couple of tourists out."

"Better not, Gramps. Squall's coming in." I spoon a mouthful of crunchy flakes into my mouth.

"Crap, I was saving for a trip to Jamaica." He gives a disgusted sigh, pushes the chair back, and stands up. He doesn't argue. He never has. He trusts my instincts implicitly.

I grin. Gramps has been saving for that Jamaican trip ever since I can remember.

"Should I batten down the hatches?"

"Wouldn't hurt anything." My head's pounding like a drum. Even the coffee doesn't help. The storm's going to be bad.

"I guess I better let my old buddies know my arthritic knee is acting up. They'll spread the word."

I nod and scoop up my cereal. Gramps' knee is legend. The number of times it has been right has garnered him respect in the fishing community.

I swallow my cereal and clear my throat. "If you see that new boy at the docks, you might let him know."

"Tyler Carlisle?"

I lift my gaze from my bowl. "You know him?"

"He likes the water," Gramps says simply. "I've run into him a time or two."

"Nothing gets past my grandparent." I raise my cup to him.

"Not if it has to do with the water. I'll be on the wharf, anyway. I'll keep an eye out for him."

"Thanks, Gramps." My tight muscles relax.

"Nice-looking young man." He picks up his cup and sips. His eyes above the rim twinkle.

Heat surges in my cheeks. "I hadn't noticed."

"Huh." His head bobs up and down as if surprised, but his lips twitch. He sets down his cup. "Well, I better get to the wharf and let everyone know what my knee is predicting."

I nod and rub my forehead.

He notices. "Headache?"

"Yeah. It's going to be intense." We both know I refer to the squall, not my aching head.

"I'll get going then."

I nod. It might not be flashy but our tag team routine saves lives. I scoop my spoon into my bowl and hit bottom. I finished my cereal without even realizing it. The chair scrapes the floor as I push up and rinse out my bowl.

I try Holly's cell again. Tyler's a teenager, surely he isn't up this early, I console myself.

"Hello." A sleepy voice answers on the other end.

I go limp with relief. "Holly, it's Piper. Is your brother there?"

"I doubt it. He was going out on his sailboat. He leaves at the crack of dawn."

"Could you reach him on his cell?' My hand tightens on the phone. Darn the boy. Hadn't I told him it was not a good day to be on the water?

"Nope. He doesn't have a booster or a mini tower."

"Okay. Thanks."

Before I can click off, Holly asks, "What's going on?" She sounds more awake.

"Gramps' knee is acting up. A sure sign bad weather is coming."

"That's nice of you to give us a heads up. But don't worry about Tyler. He's an experienced sailor."

"Good to know. I'll talk to you later."

"Since I'm up—"

I pretend not to hear and click off. Maybe Gramps is having better luck. I pour myself another cup of coffee and hit speed dial. "Gramps, any sign of Tyler?" I draw circles with the warm cup on the counter.

"I just got here. I'll call you back either way, okay?"

"Okay." The pressure at the base of my skull creeps downward. I scrub the back of my neck. Holly said he's a seasoned sailor; maybe he won't go that far out. Maybe he'll have enough time to make it home.

The minutes tick by. I pace, waiting for Gramps' call. By the time the phone rings, my head feels like a jackhammer is drilling a blast hole through my skull.

"Hello," I speak breathlessly into the mouthpiece.

"Piper, it's Holly."

Crap.

"I was wondering if you wanted to do anything today."

Impatience dances along my nerve endings like a thousand spiders. I manage to keep it out of my voice...just. "That's really nice, Holly, but I can't today. Rain check?" I'm going to be busy swimming the ocean, checking on her brother. "Just out of curiosity do you know where your brother is headed?"

"Not really. He said he didn't intend to go out too far." Before I can respond she continues, "Why the interest in my bro? Do you two have something going on?"

I pull the phone away from my ear and look at it, shocked. "Get serious, Holly. Your brother is the most popular boy in school. He can have anyone he wants. I'm the school mouse."

"The thing about mice is they can scurry around unobserved, go places, and see things that most people can't," Holly responds.

"While that's very astute on your part, I don't think that's the main thing that attracts high school boys," I reply dryly.

"You got that right." She laughs. "Though, I've never heard Tyler rhapsodize about a girl's voice before. He keeps talking about sea sirens. I hate to hurt your feelings, but I don't get it. You sound rather raspy to me. You aren't a smoker are you?"

I'd just brought my coffee to my lips when she mentions sea sirens. It goes spewing across the counter. I hastily wipe my mouth. "Listen, Holly, I've got to go. Got a call coming in."

"Okay, talk to you—"

"Yeah, sure." I click off before she can say anymore. "Come on, Gramps."

As if on cue, my cell rings. "Gramps?"

"Sorry, honey. No luck. Burt said the kid headed out a couple of hours ago."

Burt and Gramps are old cronies. They've known each other nearly sixty years.

"You're going out aren't you?"

The kitchen darkens. I lift the curtain and look out the window. The sun has disappeared and the sky is black. A wind that will quickly pick up is blowing. "Yeah. I am."

"You be careful."

"I will. And, Gramps."

"Yes?"

"You better get home."

"On my way."

I run to the bedroom and throw on a midnight blue one-piece with the back cut out then rush out the door, the screen banging behind me. I trot to the cliff's edge. The house is set off, with no near neighbors. Unless someone has a pair of binoculars focused on it, no one will see me. I dive into the foaming gray waves below.

I turn in a circle and look around. The air, heavy and still, increases the clamp-like pressure on my head.

A horizontal spear of lightning flickers along the shore. Thunder rolls. Several yards away, a speedboat skims the water's surface. Waves buck and roll in its wake. The sun that warmed the water when it came up has disappeared. I breathe in thick wet air and strike out toward sea.

Chapter 7

The wind picks up. The water rises, gray and stormy. A cold drop plops on my face then another and another.

The sky opens. Rain pours down in sheets. A large wave washes over me, picks me up, and tosses me down. I go with it, closing my nose, mouth, and blowhole. Icy water washes over and under me.

It subsides, only to build and hit again, more powerful than ever. The squall blows in earnest. I can survive this, last as long as it takes, but can Tyler?

How can his boat keep from capsizing? Somehow, I have to find him. In spite of the waves that pound me and the icy liquid that pours in my eyes, I push forward through wall after wall of gray swells.

There's nothing but an angry sea, black skies, and sheets of rain. I feel alone in the universe. The sea creatures have the good sense to head deep into the ocean and wait out the storm's ferocity.

Treading water, I glance around. To my right, something white catches my eye. I swim toward it. A wave knocks me back. I try again and get knocked back again. After what seems forever, I reach it. A poor drowned crane floats on the water. It disappears in the next gray wave.

Which direction now? I sluice the rain out of my face and push back my hair. I might as well not bother. I'm blinded almost immediately.

The waves slow. Taking advantage, I look around, cupping my hand above my eyes for better visibility. In the distance, a dot of orange catches my eye. I swim toward it, pushing through the icy water.

A dolphin DNA benefit that completely escaped me is the layer of fat under the skin to keep me warm. Right now, the only thing keeping my teeth from chattering is constant movement. Even so, goose bumps roughen my skin as I swim toward the orange dot. A swell tosses me backward. I'm getting nowhere.

I get my bearings and dive beneath the waves. Ah, much better. The ocean is rough but I'm holding my own. I press my lips together and taste the salty liquid of the sea.

I swim for about eight minutes then surface, just in time to get hit by another wave. Several feet away, something floats on the water. The downpour so intense I can't make out what it is. I swim forward, reach… and a gust of wind carries it away. I dive after it, stretching out my arm till it feels like my joints will pop. I've got it! My heart sinks. A life preserver.

"This doesn't mean it belongs to Tyler." The howling wind whips my words away.

Without the sun, it's impossible to tell what time it is. I've been in the water for hours. I'm tiring. Even girls with dolphin DNA have limits in storms.

Time to go back under. I start to dive down just as a wave lifts me eight feet in the air and tosses me down. I belly flop. "Ouch!" It hurts like a mother. Ignoring the pain, I dive below.

Rod cells in my retinas allow me to see in the murky dark of the ocean. Nothing shows above. At least the swimming isn't so difficult. Cold waves still buffet me, but not with the intensity of the surface.

I'm several miles out. I have to believe Tyler would have headed back when the squall hit or at least tried. I decide to swim horizontal with the shore for a six-mile radius from the dock. It's not perfect but it's a plan.

Back and forth. Back and forth. I'm exhausted, but I force myself on. I have no idea how long I've been in the water. My neck has a permanent crick in it from staring up at the surface.

I keep thinking of that floatation device. What if it's too late when I find him? Or worse yet, what if he's never found?

I'm so tired it takes me a moment to realize there's a shadow on the water. As I get closer, I see the outline of a boat tilted on its side. I swim faster.

There! Two long legs hang from the side of the boat, water running in rivulets along the dark hairs covering them. Pushing with my feet, I swim straight up, bubbles pouring behind me as I breathe rapidly.

I hit the surface.

It's Tyler! Barely conscious, he holds on to the side, a life preserver wrapped around his waist.

The temperature is dropping. The rain continues its steady downpour. At least the waves have died to manageable levels. I take his hands and try to pry them away from the boat. "Let go, Tyler. I'll tow you in."

Barely conscious, he blinks at me. "Piper?"

Even in the water, my body jerks. How has he recognized me? My voice.

I can't worry about that now. I grab his life vest. "Tyler, let go."

"I can't." His head lolls, his eyes close, his shoulders slump. I have no idea how long he's been in the water. I touch his hand. It's icy cold. What if he has hypothermia? Fear sluices through me.

I have to concentrate on getting him to shore.

"Let go." I paddle in place beside him.

"Can't," he repeats.

I massage the pressure points in his hands. Gradually, they open. Rain continues to fall, plastering his hair to the sides of his skull. His white cheekbones look like they will break through the skin any minute. A wave hits and knocks him several feet from the boat. I dive into the water and catch up with him in a few smooth strokes.

I surface, grab his life vest, and haul him toward shore. He floats on his back, water from the rain and waves drenching his face. I fervently hope he doesn't drown before I get him to land. Is that what waterboarding feels like?

"Tyler."

He makes no response.

"Stay with me, Tyler." I strike out faster, extending my arm as far as I can, and kick hard. Steadily, we move forward.

I feel the tremor of the wave before it reaches us. Pulling Tyler's icy body against mine, I bury his head in my shoulder. His skin is so cold it permeates my bones. I push my body close to his, trying to warm him but my own body temperature is too low.

Moments later the wave crashes over us. The powerful icy surge sucks us down. Tyler squirms against me trying to break free. I hold on, afraid he'll drown if I let go. If the wave doesn't flatten soon, he will anyway.

Finally, the wave subsides with a grumbling swish. Tyler has stopped struggling.

I head toward shore. My heart races, my breath comes in short sharp gasps. "You stay with me, Tyler. Do you hear?" I yank hard at his hair for emphasis.

"Ouch."

It's weak but I hear it.

"Piper." It's no more than a breath near my ear.

"I'm not Piper," I shout into the wind.

There's no response. I swim harder. My arms and legs ache. The sky has lightened to dull gray, still dark but not black. The rain has turned to cold drizzle. I'm exhausted. Even mutants have their limits, especially when they're hauling a limp young man through undercurrents.

I squint through the dreary mist. To my right and several hundred yards ahead is the cove. I switch direction and head toward it, praying Gramps will be waiting for me. As I get closer, I see the beam of truck lights.

My pace picks up. It has to be Gramps! There's a steep, overgrown, one-vehicle lane that circles down to the cove. It's a private road that no one else uses.

Water slaps against rock. We've made it. I hit the shallows and pull myself up on rubbery legs. I let go of Tyler's life vest and he splashes back into the water. I grab the back of his vest and haul him out.

His eyes open, dilated and unfocused. He grabs my shoulders and pulls me down against him. Shock shoots through my system. He moves a hand, brings my head down to his, and plants his mouth on mine. Not quite sure how it happens, I'm returning a kiss that has a little tongue and a lot of experience. I forget the cold and wet, lost in the moment.

He sighs. His hands fall to the wet sand. I lift my head and his flops to the side.

"Tyler?"

No response. He's passed out.

"Piper!" Gramps comes running.

"I'm okay." My cheeks hot, I hope the overcast sky and rain curtained that kiss from my grandfather's view.

"How's the boy?" Gramps hauls him away from the water, further up the rocky shore. Tyler's body bumps over pebbles and stones, till Gramps lays him on a flat spot of sand.

"I don't know."

Gramps gives me a quick look. Something in my voice must have given away my confusion: the kiss and the fear for his welfare. But I'm pretty sure he couldn't have kissed me like that if he'd been at death's door. I shudder.

Gramps sees it and mistakes it for cold. He shrugs out of his yellow slicker and drapes it around my shoulders.

"You keep it." I start to take it off.

He lays a hand on my shoulders. "Keep it, girl." He bends down awkwardly. I can almost hear old bones creak. "He's breathing."

Is he? Does it take air to kiss someone senseless?

Gramps tilts him to the side so he can cough up any water he's swallowed.

Tyler lets loose and expels what he's taken in. While Tyler wheezes, Gramps moves in front of me to block his view. He pulls the collar up around me and sticks his yellow-billed, heavy-duty, rain hat on my head, and pulls it down where my eyes are shadowed. "Let's get him in the truck."

I nod. I'm not just worried about Tyler. Gramps doesn't need to be out in the damp, chilled to the bone, at his age. In two months, he'll turn seventy-one.

He'd scoff at my concerns so I don't bother to voice them.

We each put an arm around Tyler and half-drag, half-carry him to the truck. The old door opens with a loud squawk. We lift Tyler inside. At a stiff gait, Gramps trots to the driver's side and climbs in. I hoist myself on the seat and slam the door.

Tyler's head falls against my shoulder. I have no idea whether he is conscious or has slipped back into unconsciousness. Gramps turns the key and the old truck roars to life. He reaches over and turns up the heat. The warm air blowing out the vents feels like heaven. I balance Tyler with my free arm and slouch back against the worn leather seat, my eyes closed, exhausted.

I must have drifted off because the next thing I know, Gramps is pulling me gently out of the truck. "Come on, Piper, wake up. Let's get you both inside."

I pry open sticky eyes and nod. My arms and legs feel like lead. Every bone in my body aches. Tyler shifts against me. The heat helped but he's still chilly. A shudder runs through him. His face is white, his sunken eyes stained purple.

"We need to get him in the house." The old seat groans as I shift uneasily. I slide off the seat and out of the truck.

"Piper?" Tyler's head rests on the back of the seat, his long thick lashes resting on the taut skin under his eyes.

I open my mouth to respond. Gramps shakes his head. I snap my mouth shut, appalled. What if I'd responded and he made the connection between the woman who rescued him and me?

I tug on Gramps' arm and whisper in his ear, "Do we need to take him to the hospital?"

He shakes his head and says in a low voice, "I've hauled enough men out of the sea to know he's going to be alright." Without saying another word, we drag him into the cottage and the little spare bedroom in the back. Gramps keeps his fishing rods there and I have a pen and a couple of cages for the occasional hurt turtle or bird I bring home to nurse back to health. A small sparrow, with a wing healing, chirps from his perch.

We manage to get Tyler onto the twin bed where he drops face down on the gray and white striped duvet. His long, lanky body makes the bed look even smaller.

With a grunt, Gramps rolls him over, fumbling at the clasp of the bright orange life vest Tyler still wears. I start forward to help. With an abrupt jerk of his head, Gramps motions me out of the room.

I nod and slip out. I hang up his raincoat and hat on the peg in the hallway then head for my room. Feeling fragile as cracked glass about to shatter, I head for the bathroom. There I drop my wet suit on the floor and climb into the shower. I turn the water on hot as possible and stand under it, my head down, my palms on the side of the wall. Steam that smells of vanilla-strawberry gel fills the tiny room.

I no longer feel the cold in my bones as I step out of the shower and go to my room, a soft old blue towel wrapped around me and tied above my breasts.

With a martyred sigh, I pull out baggy linen pants and one of Gramps' plaid shirts that hangs past my knees. Grimacing, I push the sleeves up and scrape back my hair. I lift the wretched glasses with all the enthusiasm I'd show a poisonous snake. Oh well, it can't be helped.

My nerd costume firmly in place, I make my way down the hall. Gramps is pulling blankets up to Tyler's chin. He straightens and motions toward the hall.

"How is he?" I whisper.

"Exhausted." Gramps takes my arm and leads me to the kitchen. He pulls eggs out of the refrigerator. With a flick of the wrist, he cracks them, the sound melding with the homey hum of the refrigerator. "He surfaced long enough to ask if you'd rescued him."

"And you said?"

"That I found him on the shore and brought him home."

"Thanks, Gramps." I heave a sigh of relief.

"Have you called his parents yet?" He beats the eggs.

"No, I thought we'd better get our stories straight first."

"You've been here all day. That's my story and I'm sticking to it." He looks over his shoulder and grins. His blues eyes twinkle like a young man's.

One look at that grin and my heart warms. He's the most important person in my universe. I refuse to think about his age or that he won't be around forever. "I like your story."

"I thought you might. You better call." He turns around and goes back to his eggs.

"Will do. By the way, what time is it?"

He glances at his watch. "Two-thirty."

"In the afternoon?" No way. I'd been in the water, in the middle of a storm for almost six hours. But then again, so had Tyler. Who knew when his catamaran turned over.

"That's right." Our eyes meet. The worry he felt surfaces before it's quickly hidden.

Trying for reassuring, I wink at him.

He winks back. "While you were out there, I kept thinking of the night you were born. There was a gale blowing then, too, and the rain coming down hard enough it washed the roads out. Good thing your daddy and momma decided to have you at home. We wouldn't have been able to get out anyway." His face softens as he speaks and his lips turn up in a reminiscent smile.

"Having Grams deliver me was a good decision." I grin and point over my shoulder to my blowhole.

"Neither of your parents knew how much of your momma's DNA you carried and didn't want to take any chances with anyone outside the family. But that's ancient history. You best make that phone call."

"Right." Lifting myself from the chair, I trot to my room, groaning as my creaky legs complain. I scoop my cell phone off the dresser and hit speed dial.

"Hello." Holly's voice sounds strained.

"Holly, it's Piper. I wanted to let you know, your brother is all right."

"Thank God! Where is he?"

Before I can respond, she sings out, "Mom, Dad, he's all right."

"Sorry. Where is he, Piper?"

"Here."

"At your place?"

"Yes."

"How'd he get there? What happened?"

"I have no idea. He's asleep so I haven't been able to find anything out. The only thing I know is Gramps said he found him on the shore." I cross my fingers with my free hand. I'm such a bad liar.

"On the shore?"

"Yeah, pretty wild huh?"

"I'll say, but he's all right?" I can feel anxiety thrumming through the phone.

"I think so, Holly. To be on the safe side, your parents might want to take him to emergency and have him checked out. Gramps says he's going to be fine, but it wouldn't hurt to confirm it."

"I'll pass the suggestion along. We'll be right there. And, Piper?"

"Yeah?"

"Thanks. We owe you."

"You don't owe me a thing." I end the connection before she can say anything more. Thanks of any sort embarrass me.

My stomach rumbles, reminding me how hungry I am. When I enter the kitchen, the aroma of fresh brewed coffee wraps around my senses like a lover's embrace. Gramps stands at the stove stirring a pot. He's been a busy bee.

"How do you think he is?" I pull out two plain mugs and pour a cup for each of us, so tired my hand shakes.

"He'll be all right. He's young and strong. Sleep will do wonders for him. Sit down and I'll bring you some oatmeal."

"Thanks." My chair scrapes against the white oak floorboards as I pull it out and fall into it. I lift my cup then take a sip. Even the rich-flavored caffeine does no more than give me enough energy to eat the huge bowl of oatmeal Gramps thumps down in front of me, followed by a plateful of fluffy yellow eggs and light brown toast.

It's a toss-up whether my rumbling stomach or my dragging fatigue will win out. My stomach wins by a hair. I inhale the eggs and toast, scrape the oatmeal bowl clean then stumble to my bed where I throw myself face down on the soft pink coverlet. *I should check on Tyler* is my last waking thought.

The screech of a gull wakes me. The room is lighter than when I fell into bed. Maybe the sun has come out. I tumble out of bed, pull back the curtain, and blink. The sky is a contented blue without a cloud and the sun shines bright in the eastern sky. I've slept through the day and night.

Hastily, I throw on my clothes, tuck my hair in a ball cap, push my glasses up onto the bridge of my nose, and trot down the hallway to the little guest room.

I open the door a slit and peek in. The sparrow chirps and ruffles its good wing. The bed is empty. The gray and white duvet smoothed neatly over it.

I make a quick trip through the cottage. Tyler is gone and so is Gramps. Though Gramps has at least left a pot of coffee for me. Still feeling slightly fragile, I doctor it with cream and sugar.

Taking one last look to make sure Tyler isn't around, I wander back to my bedroom nursing my cream-laden java. Once in my room, I toss off the glasses, let my hair down, comb it with my fingers, and step out of my nerd attire, leaving the offending garments on the floor where they fall.

From my closet, I pull out a red-ribbed, sleeveless, fitted-tee and white shorts. I grab a bottle of Crimson Sunset nail polish, and carrying my coffee in the other hand, go to the small deck on the back of the house.

Listening to the happy chirp of birds, and the rhythmic lap of the waves, I paint my toenails, sip my coffee, and fall asleep.

"Piper. Mr. Dunn. Piper. Mr. Dunn." I'm dreaming of Tyler. Telling him, even though he's a great kisser, I can't get involved with him. Along with the pounding, the voice becomes more insistent. Groggy, I open my eyes then jerk upright. "Oh, my God, it is Tyler."

I leap out of the chair, run into the house, and throw on my nerd gear. Out of breath, I race to the door. He's turning away. The old screen creaks when I open it. "What are you doing here?"

He turns and gives me a mega-powered smile that leaves my knees weak. "Shouldn't you be home in bed?" I manage.

"I'm okay. Can I come in?"

"Sure." I step back.

He stops inside the threshold. His first words take me by surprise. "You paint your toenails."

Heat floods my cheeks. "So?"

"So, you have attractive feet."

"Gramps said you nearly drowned. Your brain must still be waterlogged." I try hard not to squirm.

"Possibly," he admits. "But that has no bearing on the fact that you've got nice feet. They're slender and perfectly formed."

"Carlisle, do you have a foot fetish?" I narrow my eyes.

He laughs and seems sincerely amused. "No. It's just that's one of the few portions of your anatomy that's visible."

I hate these clothes. "You need to be home resting. You had a harrowing experience. I'm surprised your parents let you out of the house."

"I snuck out."

"You need to go back home and to bed." I open the door.

Instead of walking through it, he leans against the wall, crosses his arms, and looks at me speculatively. "I do feel rather weak. Maybe I should lie down."

I glance at him uneasily. These glasses make it difficult to see. But it doesn't take too much effort to recognize the devils dancing in his eyes. "You certainly aren't suggesting…"

"What?" he asks innocently, the devils still dancing "I'm just saying if you're worried about me I can rest here."

I heave a sigh and try to get my racing heart under control. I do my best to act put out. "You better go home."

"I can't help teasing you. You're so easy to get a rise out of."

"I knew that. There's no way you'd want to go to bed with me." The bitterness in my voice embarrasses me.

He takes a step closer. "You're wrong about that," he responds, suddenly serious.

I take a step back.

"But what I came for is to thank you and your grandfather for saving my life. You especially." His gaze burns into mine.

I reach for the doorknob. "Gramps isn't here. I'll give him the message. But as far as me, I didn't do anything." I hold crossed-fingers behind my back.

"If you don't mind, I'll wait for your grandfather." He says nothing about my involvement or lack thereof.

I sigh and motion him toward the small living room. "If you won't leave," I say ungraciously, "you might as well sit down. Would you like some tea?" I would offer other beverages, but I don't like his color. He looks feverish and needs to be off his feet.

"Yes, thank you."

"Sit." I point in the direction of our living room. It holds a saggy old couch and a TV that still has a tube instead of the sleek LCDs.

"Yes, ma'am." He salutes me and heads toward the living room.

I walk into the kitchen and heat the water. When the teakettle begins to whistle, I pour the boiling water over the tea bags then set the kettle back on the stove. Turning, I nearly land in Tyler's arms. The sun shines through the kitchen window and casts a shadow across his face.

He places one hand on the counter and one on the cool portion of the stovetop, neatly trapping me in the corner. My heart pounds. I lift my chin and ask in what I hope is a cool voice, "What are you doing?"

"When I was in the water, a beautiful young woman rescued me. What do you know about that?"

"Maybe you hallucinated. That doesn't sound possible, especially in that storm."

"My sister told me you called continually trying to get hold of me to tell me not to go out. You knew a storm was coming before anyone else, even the weather station. How?"

I had an answer for that one. "Gramps' knee. It always acts up when bad weather's coming."

"I'll give you that one. But how did I get to shore?"

"How should I know?"

"Oh, I think you know all right. And I know how to prove it," he murmurs, his lips a breath away from mine.

Chapter 8

I expect him to go for my glasses and plan accordingly. But the sneaky boy angles his head below them and kisses me with the same expertise as before. My breath catches as he kisses the corner of my mouth then nips at the fleshy part of my lip before his tongue finds mine. The heat radiating from him takes on scorching proportions. My body limp, I cling to him.

The next moment, my swirling world coheres into one sharp sizzle of electricity and I kiss him back for all I'm worth.

I have no previous experience, his kiss yesterday my first, but I'm nothing if not a quick learner. I press against his hard frame and cooperate enthusiastically. I move my hands from his shoulder and wrap one in his thick silky mane of hair.

His breath quickens and he slides his fingertips along the side of my breast. I moan and lean in. His hot fingers slide under my top and caress my skin, scorching wherever they touch. He lowers them and cups my butt with both hands, pulling me hard against his body. Things are well on the way to getting out of control when he groans, drops his hands, and steps back.

He stares at me wild-eyed. The pulse in his neck is jumping. With unsteady hands, he reaches for my glasses. Reflexively, I slap his hands.

"I kissed you yesterday."

I bite my lips together and take a moment to settle my thundering heart. "No, you didn't."

"You're the most beautiful thing I've ever seen." His gaze does a slow slide over me trying to pierce through the clothes to the body below. He frowns. "I remember eyes of an unusual shade." He snaps his fingers and smiles in triumph. "Turquoise. You have turquoise eyes. Why do you dress like that? Why hide those eyes? Are you afraid every boy in school will have cardiac arrest if they see you?" he jokes.

All I can do is brazen it out. "I don't have a clue what you're talking about. Have you seen a doctor yet, Carlisle? You must have hit your head when you went over. It's causing you to hallucinate."

He picks up my hands and plays with my fingers. "You can trust me, you know." His voice is gentle, his eyes sincere.

The touch of his hands on mine nearly has me forgetting years of caution. *I'm a mutant.* The words hover on my tongue. The only way I can suppress them is too bite down. "Ouch!" The pain has me pulling my hands away and clamping one over my mouth.

"Are you all right?" His head tips forward and his eyebrows draw together.

"Fine. I bit my tongue," I mumble behind my hand. "Really, I think you'd better go."

"I was hoping to thank your grandpa."

I know a stall when I hear one. "I'll tell him for you." I nudge him toward the door.

"No need." He gives me that quirky grin that has the strangest effect on my pulse. Not to mention the pull in the pit of my tummy. "I'll be back to thank him myself."

My head drops momentarily in defeat. I sigh.

He leans in and kisses my forehead. The touch is as gentle as a butterfly kiss. "You can trust me, Piper." Then, he's gone.

"What, oh what, am I going to do?" My head in my hands, I stumble back to the patio and slump down in the lounge chair. I draw up my legs, wrap my arms around them, and drop my chin on my knees. This is exactly why I avoid involvement of any kind. "The sea creatures I rescue never hassle me. They don't care what I look like," I grouse.

The screen door creaks. "Talking to yourself, Pip?" Gramps asks. He trudges out favoring his right knee. The one the arthritis is the worst in.

"Tyler was here." Glum, I take off the offending glasses and run my fingers through my hair.

"Oh?" Gramps arches bushy white brows and waits.

"He wanted to thank you."

"A polite young man. I like that." He nods. "Anything else?"

"He'll probably be back to thank you himself." I heave a defeated sigh and twist a wisp of hair near my face.

"You don't sound in favor of that." Gramps grimaces and shifts in the chair he's just lowered himself into. He picks up his knee and straightens it.

"He knows." In direct contrast to my gloomy mood, the setting sun is bright and warm. A squirrel, more in tune with my frame of mind, sits in a nearby tree, twitching its tail and complaining.

"I see. What are you going to do?"

"What I've already done. Deny."

"How did he make the connection?"

Heat sweeps my face. I twist my fingers, my head down. "He kissed me."

"Quite an enterprising young man. He figured it out from a simple little kiss?"

Simple? Right. My chest rises and falls. I heave a deep sigh. "He kissed me in the water. Then he kissed me in the kitchen. He's convinced I'm the girl that rescued him."

"That does complicate things." Gramps rubs his knee. A seagull flies overhead crying in a harsh voice. For an instant, I wish I could join him in flight. I shake off the notion and straighten my shoulders. Piper Dunn, aka super-mutant, doesn't run from trouble.

Gramps breaks into my thoughts. "Is he trustworthy?"

I whirl in my chair. "I can't tell him. I can't tell anyone."

"I know, Pip, I know. But I won't be around forever. I'd like to know there's someone who'd take care of you when I'm gone, someone you can rely on."

My body turns to ice. "Don't talk like that. You're going to be around a long time." I force a laugh. "Besides, you think an eighteen-year-old boy could take care of me?"

"I was nineteen when I married your grandmother. That's a year older than Tyler."

Had I known that? I turn and look at him, my head cocked. "Yeah, but you were mature." I wiggle my eyebrows and grin.

"Of course I was." He lifts his chin then tips it and winks at me.

My cell phone rings. I grab it in relief. "Excuse me." I jump up and head for the kitchen. The phone's display makes me groan: from the frying pan to the fire. "Hello, Holly."

"Oh, Piper. I want to thank you and your grandfather for saving Tyler."

I heave a sigh. "I didn't do anything. It was Gramps."

"Whatever. My parents and I are very appreciative. Dad towed Tyler's boat in. Once he gets it cleaned up, we'd like to take you and your grandpa on a picnic to one of the nearby islands.

"I still can't figure out how Tyler made it to shore. It's nothing short of a miracle. He doesn't remember a thing. You know," her voice rises in excitement, "I wonder if a dolphin got him to shore. You hear about that stuff all the time. Piper? Piper, are you all right?"

"Sorry, something caught in my throat," I choke out. Yeah, a dolphin helped him all right. A mutant dolphin.

"So he said he can't remember anything?"

"Yeah, weird huh? He says he doesn't remember anything till he woke up at your house."

I breathe a sigh of relief. Tyler hasn't sold me out. "How's he doing?"

"He snuck out of the house for a while. He got back a few minutes ago. Mom made him go straight to bed. He's planning on going to school tomorrow. Speaking of which, I got homework. I'll see you then."

"Bye." I shove my phone in my pocket and wander into the bedroom to do my own homework. By the time the first stars come out, I'm finished and ready to check out my piece of the ocean.

I put on a copper-colored swimsuit then track down Gramps, in front of the television watching his favorite police drama. "I'm going out for a swim."

"Be careful, the waves are still high."

"Will do. Can I fix you a bite to eat before I go?"

"Nope. I think I'll just reheat some leftovers. I can wait for you, if you don't think you'll be gone long."

"No need. Though, I won't plan on staying out unless I run into something."

He nods, his attention already back on the show.

I walk over and kiss him on the cheek. What he'd said today about not being around forever scares me. There's no need to point out, or linger on, the obvious. But, if and when something happens to Gramps, my whole world will collapse. My eyes well up. I turn and hurry out the door.

I trot down the little dirt path till I reach the tip of the cliff and dive off. Gramps is right. The waves are up. I gasp then close my mouth as I go deeper than expected, the water shocking me. I swim to the surface, push my hair out of my eyes, and chuff to open my blowhole.

Finding the waves' rhythm, I begin to swim. Other than being high, everything seems calm. Blue ripples into turquoise. The waves enfold me like a mother's arms. I roll over and over out of sheer joy. I swim about a mile out and follow the shoreline, my turf.

I've been in the water around an hour. Everything appears calm. I turn to head home when I hear the distressed sound of a turtle. I swim toward the noise in the cool dark. Stars wink in the sky and glitter on the water.

A shark passes me but pays no mind. Its fin causes a silver ripple on the surface.

The noise grows weaker. I swim faster. A glimmer of movement catches my eye. A sea turtle is tangled in a fish net and slowly drowning. Under normal circumstances, a turtle can last hours under water before surfacing for air, but the stress of being caught in the net is quickly using up the creature's oxygen supply. I pull a knife out of the scabbard strapped to my leg and cut the net.

Hundreds of shrimp scuttle to safety. The turtle tries to swim but her strength is gone. She begins to drop. I grab her fin and push toward the surface. I can see the moon's reflection glistening on the waves just before I break through the water.

I get my arms around the hard wet shell and push upward. For many minutes, the turtle remains motionless. I wonder if I'm too late. Finally, her legs begin to move. I let go. She gives me a head butt of thanks before swimming away.

"Oof."

Happy, I breathe in air, chuff, then dive down. I take one more turn around the bay before I head home. The night sky is filled with stars that spill out sparkling shards of light. But even without them the rod cells in my retinas give me better vision than most humans. Even so, it's not until I pull myself out of the water and stand wringing out my hair that I see him.

Chapter 9

He stands in shadows, but I'd know him anywhere. His form is as familiar to me as my own.

What to do? Pretend I haven't seen him and take the trail to the house as I normally do? Or go back in the ocean and not surface till he leaves? I opt for door number two. I turn and walk into the surf.

"There's no need. I'm leaving." His pitched voice carries over the restless, lapping waves.

I force myself to keep going. The muscles tighten as I fight the urge to look over my shoulder. I dive into the water and swim straight out. Paddling, I turn and look back. He's gone.

I wait another twenty minutes before I head in. This time, I scrutinize the shore before I get out. I don't see him. I pull myself out of the water and trot quickly up the trail to the house. When I get to the top, I look around. No, Tyler. I blow out a sigh of relief and trot to the house.

"Damn it, is he stalking me?" I mumble under my breath.

The screen door creaks, Gramps calls out, "Pip, is that you?"

"Yup, it's me."

He comes to the entryway, a newspaper tucked under his arm. Gramps is always reading a newspaper. He reads at least five different papers a day. He's probably better versed on economics and world events than most college professors.

"Any critters in trouble tonight?"

We head for the kitchen.

"I freed a sea turtle from another one of those blasted fishing nets. I thought she'd drown before I got to her. But she's fine."

"Good for you."

I stick my head in the refrigerator, pull out a chocolate cake I'd made earlier in the week and a carton of milk. "Want a piece?" I shut the door with my foot.

"Your cake? Sure."

He gets a couple of plates, glasses, and forks. While he pours the milk, I cut us big slices.

"I've got to tell you, you're making a lot of fishermen mighty unhappy." He sits down and shovels a large forkful of the moist, dark dessert into his mouth.

I take a big bite myself and answer with difficulty, "Can't be helped."

"I know, love."

I chug cold milk then set the glass down. "Tyler was hanging around the beach when I came in."

"What did you do?" He sets down his fork, waiting for my response.

"Headed back in the water. He called out it wasn't necessary, he was leaving."

Gramps raises his eyebrows. "Did he?"

"Yes."

"What are you going to do, honey?"

"Keep denying I'm me." I sigh and make swirls of the crumbs on my plate with the fork.

He pats me on the shoulder and picks up my plate and fork. "It's a knotty problem, but things have a way of working out."

As he puts the plates in the sink, I walk up behind him and hug him, putting my cheek against his back. "Love you, Gramps."

"You too, Pip. Now you better get to bed. You've got school tomorrow."

The rooster-shaped clock on the wall shows five minutes till ten. "Gosh, I'll get nearly seven hours sleep tonight."

"That's pretty good for you."

"Darn right it is. Sleep tight, Gramps."

"Don't let the bedbugs bite."

I grin as I walk out of the kitchen.

Once in my room, I wriggle into a mint green cami and undies, and plop onto the bed. I take a moment to wiggle my toes and admire my polish before I crawl under the sheets.

My eyes determinedly closed, I court sleep. Slumber eludes me. I try counting sheep but at one hundred and one, I'm still awake. I switch to lines from Romeo and Juliet. My body grows heavy and my mind wanders. I'm kissing Romeo, who bears a striking resemblance to Tyler. As Tyler-Romeo tells me, "O, then, dear saint, let lips do what hands do," Mercutio begins to sing and Friar Lawrence plays an electric guitar.

My eyes fly open. I sit straight up in bed and fumble with the button on the alarm to turn off the power pop song blaring on the radio. I guess I slept after all.

I stumble to the bathroom, brush my teeth with minty toothpaste before taking a quick shower. I stand in front of the mirror and comb my hair. Pale gleaming strands fly around my shoulders and accentuate my turquoise eyes. My lashes are long and thick but need mascara to darken them. I sigh. What difference does it make? No one is going to see them other than Gramps.

I ruthlessly pull my hair back and contain it in a scrunchie before I stick pins in it and make it into a bun. Even though it's protective covering, I still hate it. I trudge into my bedroom and pull on my clothes.

I manage to find a short-sleeved, shapeless cotton hoodie. I bought a gray one, a drab olive, and a mustard yellow. I pull on the yellow, knowing from experience it drains any possible color from my face. I also manage to find gray-muslin pants that tie at the waist with a drawstring.

Since I bought them two sizes too big, I have to roll the legs up several times and even with the drawstring drawn tight, continuously haul them back up to my waist. I grab my repugnant pink glasses, and head down the hall.

I follow breakfast scents to the kitchen where a bowl of oatmeal topped with apples and raisins sits at the table along with a cup of steaming coffee.

I slump into the chair and take a quick sip. My eyes close and I whimper as I savor the hot, rich-tasting caffeine. My world rights. "Thanks, Gramps."

"No problem, baby girl. How'd you sleep?"

No point in going there. I do what any right-thinking granddaughter would do: I lie. "Like a log. You?"

He places a bowl across from me and lowers himself into the chair. "The same."

Having just lied myself, I find it easy to hear the hearty, false ring in his voice. I look at him and frown. He has bags under his eyes and his skin has a pallor that concerns me. I set down my cup. Coffee splashes on the cheery, yellow flowered placemat. "Are you all right?" I lean forward to study him closer.

"Of course, I'm all right. I should have gone to bed earlier that's all."

I press my lips together. Come rain or shine, unless he's waiting up for me, Gramps is in bed by ten-thirty. He watches the ten o'clock news then lights out. If the snores I hear whenever I pass his bedroom are anything to go by, most of the time he sleeps like a baby.

"Let me make an appointment for you with Doc Johnson."

"That old quack? I don't think so."

"How about his partner," I ask rather desperately.

"I'm fine," he says firmly. "Just a little indigestion. Once this oatmeal lines my stomach, I'll be good to go. Now, you eat, girl." He waves his spoon at me.

Beneath lowered lashes, I keep an eye on him. After a few minutes, his color does seem to improve.

"Stop staring and eat your oatmeal." Gramps doesn't look up from his newspaper.

I'd roll my eyes but he'd see that through his forehead as well.

After I suck down my oatmeal, I grab my book bag and glasses, give Gramps a quick kiss and dash out the door.

Humming, I drive down the hill, my monster truck belching smoke and rumbling like a demon. When I pull in the school lot, I'm almost disappointed Fahrenbacher isn't there. It would be worth the crap I'd take from the asshole to watch him turn white when I park Beulah, the monster truck, next to his sports car...again.

A couple of pieces of rust crumble from Beulah's frame when I slam the door. I trot into Rosemont High and reach lit class with seconds to spare. Surprisingly, there's an empty seat by Tyler. But I keep going and pretend not to see him smile at me.

As I slide into my seat and plop my bag onto the tablet arm, the bell rings. Holly rushes in, yanks me out of my seat, and whirls me in a circle. "Thank you."

My face hot, I drop into my seat. She plops down beside me.

"Ladies, a little decorum if you please. This is English Lit, not a contact sport." Miss Sweeney smiles when she says it, taking the sting out of it.

The students titter. Though, in a subdued manner since everyone is still half-asleep and Holly's a favorite.

My face flames, but nothing bothers Holly.

"I'm sorry, Miss Sweeney, but I couldn't contain myself."

I know what's coming. *Don't say it, Holly.*

"Piper and her grandfather saved my brother's life this weekend."

A murmur of excitement rises in the room.

I'm ready to die of sheer embarrassment. I glance at Tyler. He looks about as thrilled as I do with his twin's announcement.

Miss Sweeney glances at my heated face and takes pity on me. "That's very laudable indeed, but shall we get down to the business at hand?"

Works for me.

Sandra Cox

I force myself to keep my attention on Miss Sweeney and not let my gaze slide to Tyler. Other than half a dozen times, I succeed. Even though he's two rows up, he still manages to turn around and intercept a couple of my glances. I trust he can't tell I'm looking at him through these disgusting glasses.

When the bell rings, I jump up. My plan: to beat both the Carlisle twins out the door.

I have to step over Holly, but since several girls are already flocking around her, I make good my escape. Tyler also has his entourage. But he must manage to fight his way through, because I'm barely out the door when he catches up to me.

"She was just trying to help, you know."

"How do you figure?" Clutching my book bag, I rush down the hall.

"She wants people to know how brave you are."

I skid to a stop. With a bit of difficulty, Tyler does the same. Seething, I poke my finger into his chest. "I just want to be left alone. Is that so hard?" I know he's right, Holly meant no harm, quite the opposite. But she has no idea what's at stake. My life is on the line. I can't get close to people. If anyone discovers what I am and blabs it, I'll end up like my mom, a lab rat. Locked away like an animal.

He takes my finger and instead of dropping it, holds it. His gaze tries to penetrate my hideous glasses. I can't believe he has much luck there. "Why, Piper? Why do you want to be left alone?"

His gentleness almost undoes me. I snatch my hand back. "Just stay away from me." I slam down the hall and jerk the locker door open with unnecessary force.

"Well, well, well, if it's not the clumsy nerd."

And the hits just keep on coming. I turn, ready for a fight. My legs planted, my chin up, I bare my teeth. "What do you want, Fahrenbacher?"

"Oh, the little nerd has a backbone." A couple of his buddies snicker.

If I have an angel on one shoulder and a devil on the other, the devil's winning, while the angel is wringing her hands, shushing me. "A backbone and a brain, which is more than I can say for you, dumbass." I lift my chin and fist my hands. I have no idea what I intend to do. Edgar is built like a meat locker.

An ugly molten-red suffuses his face. Before I can add any more witticisms, he picks me up, shoves me in my locker, and slams it shut with me inside.

I open my mouth to snarl. Before I have a chance to scream invectives at Edgar the Asshole, a voice stops me in mid-breath.

"Let her out of the locker."

"This doesn't concern you, Carlisle."

"The hell it doesn't. Let her out, Edgar."

"If I don't?"

"You and I are going to dance. After school, in the park where there won't be any faculty to interrupt us."

I stare through the slits of the locker door. Tyler has never raised his voice. But the expression on his face turns my blood cold. His eyes are flat, his fists clenched. My mad is gone. Concern for Tyler has taken its place. If his body language is anything to go by, I'm more afraid of his kicking Fahrenbacher's ass and getting in trouble for it than getting his own tail whipped.

Then I remember his weekend ordeal. *Crap.* I bite back a moan and ring my hands. For once, I'm smart enough to keep my mouth shut. It doesn't take a genius to realize interference from me is the last thing Tyler wants.

Fahrenbacher shrugs and opens the door. "I didn't realize you and the little geek are an item."

"The park at four o'clock. Be there." Expression grim, Tyler plucks me out of the locker.

"What's your problem, Carlisle? I let the geek out."

"Maybe I just don't like you, Fahrenbacher." Tyler's voice is soft, his body relaxed, but tension pours off him in waves.

Fahrenbacher shrugs. "It's your ass."

"Don't worry about mine."

Fahrenbacher smirks. He turns and saunters away, saying something to the two groupies following him that causes them to laugh. One guy looks at me then at Tyler, a puzzled expression on his face. He shakes his head.

I understand his dilemma. Why is the hottest boy in school with me? I close my eyes and mentally correct myself. Tyler isn't with me. But for whatever reason he's taken it on himself to protect me.

Showing my appreciation, I grab his arm and shriek, "Are you insane?"

He takes mine, pulls it through his, and begins to walk in the direction of study hall.

I'm too overset to pull away. "What do you think you're doing? You can't fight Fahrenbacher."

"This has to stop. You don't rationalize with someone like Fahrenbacher."

"You can't do this. I don't doubt you're good"—I ignore that brief moment when the confidence he radiated convinced me he could take

Fahrenbacher—"but Fahrenbacher is built like a tree. His biceps look like footballs."

He clasps his heart. "Your confidence unmans me." He gives me that quirky smile that normally distracts me, but for once, I'm too rattled to notice.

I grab his arm again. "Please, don't do this."

He stops and plays with my fingers. "This is the only language he knows or respects. I not only intend to kick his ass, I intend to show you how so when I'm not around, if someone messes with you, you can take them. You aren't going to end up in a locker again." The expression on his face has me stepping back.

He sees it and immediately relaxes. "Come on, you'll be late for study hall."

"You can't do this. You nearly drowned. And even if you hadn't, I don't need or want you to fight my battles." I face him, my book bag pressed against my chest, all but gnashing my teeth.

"Want it or not you've got it." He turns on his heel and heads for his class. I slink into study hall.

There's a low buzz of excitement as I walk in. *Great.* So much for anonymity. I keep my head down in hopes no one will try to hold a conversation with me. Since no one normally speaks to me, it isn't an issue.

I can hear the whispers and feel the speculative stares. One of the cuter girls I've seen flirting her head off with Tyler says, in a voice impossible to miss, "What's he see in her anyhow?"

"You're just jealous, Chris, because he doesn't pay any attention to you." I recognize the voice of one of Holly's friends, who's started nodding and smiling when she sees me in the hall.

"That just goes to show what you know. Tyler most certainly does pay attention to me," Chris spits out.

"Meow, meow," A boy two rows over calls out. The rest of the students laugh. The hall monitor walks in and the class reluctantly refocuses.

Fifty minutes later the bell rings. I jump up as if my pants are on fire and shoot out the door, not that the hall is much better. Holly comes toward me, a look of consternation on her face. "Is it true?"

No point in playing dumb, I nod.

"My brother, the idiot."

I nod again. At last, a kindred spirit.

"What is he thinking?" she wails.

"Like I have a clue. Does he do this sort of thing often?"

"Never."

"Why is he now?"

"My understanding is it has something to do with Fahrenbacher stuffing you in a locker."

My face flames. "Well, I can't say that was fun but it's no reason to become a human punching bag."

"We spent one summer with my cousin. It was educational." She smiles and waves at one of the cheerleaders who hurries past her. The cheerleader waves back with a toothy smile.

"I'm happy for you. Does it have any bearing on the matter at hand?"

Holly giggles. "Oh, yeah."

We head for Spanish Class with me no wiser.

The day passes way too fast. Why couldn't it move this quickly any other day? I don't see any more of Tyler. I have a feeling he's avoiding me.

When the bell rings, Holly and I join the mass exodus heading for the park two blocks away. The only students who are going to miss the fight are those in detention and I wouldn't be surprised if they cut out.

I toss my bag in my truck so my hands will be free to wring. I want to wail like a banshee but bite my lips together to keep from it and bite my tongue in the process.

There's a small clearing on the far side of the park, hidden from view by a row of pines. We get there in time to see Fahrenbacher and Tyler circle each other. They wear jeans and undershirts, their shirts and books tossed casually near the base of a tree. Holly and I elbow our way to the front.

Fahrenbacher flexes his muscles and makes me flinch. They're as thick as a body builder's. I look at Tyler and sigh. He's just so darn pretty. I only hope he's half as pretty when this is over.

Tyler's triceps are partially hidden by his tee. He raises his arm to flick a lock of hair off his face. The sleeve rolls toward his shoulder. Though half the size of Fahrenbacher's, the smooth skin looks muscled and firm. Maybe he stands a chance. *Please, God.*

Tyler flexes his legs and makes a beckoning motion. Fahrenbacher charges him and Tyler steps nimbly aside. Again, Fahrenbacher comes at him. Tyler sidesteps him, his movements as fluid as water. I breathe easier. Maybe he won't get creamed after all.

"Stop dancing like a girl and hold still." Fahrenbacher growls.

Tyler shows teeth. You can't really call it a smile.

This time when Fahrenbacher charges, Tyler steps to the side and swings out with his leg, catching his opponent on the thigh.

Fahrenbacher stumbles, turns and swings wild.

"He's playing with him." Holly shifts to the right for a better view.

"Who's playing with whom?" I shift with her.

"Isn't it obvious?"

"Not from here it's not."

Tyler pivots on his heel and kicks backward, catching Fahrenbacher in the gut with his foot. When Fahrenbacher doubles over, Tyler whirls and clips him on the jaw and he crumples.

Tyler stands poised on the balls of his feet, his fists clenched. Fahrenbacher shakes his head and lumbers to his feet. He lunges and grabs Tyler in a deadly embrace, squeezing.

Hunching his shoulders, Tyler puts his hands together and brings them straight up, breaking the embrace, then claps his hands against Fahrenbacher's ears. I squint. It looks like he's holding back.

Fahrenbacher staggers like a drunken sailor. It doesn't look like Tyler exerted himself at all.

His fists raised, Edgar the Asshole shakes his head.

"Quit playing with him, Tyler, and finish it," Holly mutters.

I glance at her out of the corner of my eye but can't keep my gaze from her brother. As if he heard her—they are twins after all—he twists his hip, throws out his right arm and clips Fahrenbacher on the jaw.

Fahrenbacher's eyes roll back in his head and he goes down.

One of Edgar's buddies races forward. He taps Edgar on the face. "Come on. Wake up."

Edgar moans and starts to sit up.

With the exception of myself and Holly, the crowd surges forward. The guys clap Tyler on the back and the girls ooh and ahh. I shake my head and turn to Holly. "How'd he do that?"

"Let's go to the Cat and grab a latte. I'll tell you all about it."

We trudge in silence, both of us lost in our own thoughts. Since we're the first to leave, we beat the inevitable crowd. Everyone else must have the same idea. By the time we grab a booth, the place is filling up.

I take a long sip of the iced caffeine-laden chocolate beverage and begin to feel better. My heart has quit thumping like a jackhammer and my pulse rate is almost back to normal.

"Okay, give." I lean back against the wooden bench.

Holly lifts her straw and licks off the whip cream. She plunges it back in her drink and takes a long sip then sighs with pleasure.

Impatient, I shift on the bench.

"Has Tyler ever talked much about our family?"

"Uh, no. Is there a connection here?" I wrinkle my brow, confused.

She laughs. "Yeah. He spent one summer with our cousins in Chicago. He learned a lot about street fighting." She grins.

"Ah."

At that moment, the noise level rises. Excited chatter breaks out around us. I don't need to look to know who's walked in.

I wait till he and his retinue move to the front to order then surge to my feet. "Holly, hate to drink and run, but I've got to get going. See ya tomorrow."

"Bwak, bwa, bwa, bwak, bwak." Holly tucks her hands into her armpits and flaps them, making chicken sounds.

"Sticks and stones, etc. etc." I turn and flee.

Chapter 10

Beulah grumbles, spouting smoke as I push for more speed. I need the ocean. It's the only thing that can calm me, give me peace. Cool water pulling at my body, surging and pulsing around me. I can almost feel the waves beckoning me; hear the soft murmur of the sea. I press harder on the pedal and Beulah wheezes up the slope.

I pull to a stop in a cloud of dust. White smoke from the tailpipe pollutes the environment. Gramps' truck is not in sight. He's probably down at the docks. I hop out and run into the house. In my room, I shed my nerd apparel down to a hot-pink two-piece. I often wear my two pieces under my outfits so when I shuck my clothes, I'm ready to rock and roll.

I leave a note for Gramps affixed to the fridge, let myself out of the house, and trot to the cliff's edge and dive.

Tension lifts the moment I'm in the water. I watch the glorious play of colors as sunlight glistens on the surface and lightens the water.

Everything's okay. As long as I can swim, I can survive.

Something smooth and cold nudges my belly. Startled, I pull up my feet and glance down. A dolphin grins at me and chatters. I chatter back. She swims beside me, brushing me gently with her body. I grab her fin and swim alongside, letting her pull me.

We play this game for a while. Two larger dolphins join us and begin to chirp. With a nudge of her nose, the smaller dolphin leaves me to join her parents. I wave at her. She flicks her tail at me.

I exhale and smile. Bubbles roll out of my mouth. She's just what I needed.

I take a quick swim through the cove, looking around while I dog paddle. I don't see anyone and head to shore. Water streaming from my body, I stand and wring out my hair. The setting sun warms my shoulders and throws a red glow on the waves.

Scrunching sand between my toes, I head toward the path that leads to our house.

I'm almost to the pathway when he steps out from behind the ancient Douglas fir that grows next to the dirt track.

Chapter 11

"How long are you going to keep screwing with me?" Tyler's hands are shoved into a black windbreaker, his cheeks flushed as if he's running a fever.

Holy Shit. Fear momentarily freezes me. It quickly turns to sizzling anger. How dare he track me down like an FBI agent looking for someone on the most wanted list? I clench my fists. It takes everything I have not to take a swing. All I'd get from that would be broken knuckles, though the fantasy of doing some damage is tantalizing.

I uncurl my fingers, force myself to relax, and arch my eyebrows. "Do I know you?" I change the timbre of my voice, make it higher. It strains my throat.

He blinks and looks confused. Then his lips relax and he shakes his head. "Nice try, but I'm not buying it."

"I'm afraid you've mistaken me for someone else." *Damn him. Damn him. Damn him.* Why has he pushed this and put me in this situation? I force myself to relax.

"Yeah, I sure have. With a classmate who hides behind shapeless clothes and glasses. But I'm pretty sure I know how to straighten out the confusion."

He reaches out and pulls me into his arms. His warm lips cover mine, gentle but thorough. I rest against him, enjoying the pull in my stomach and the tingle that runs down to my toes.

The cry of a gull overhead brings me back to my senses. I push against him. It isn't much of a shove but he lets me go.

"Yup, you most certainly are Piper."

I go from sexual tension to pulse-pounding rage in seconds. Hands fisted on hips, my chest heaving, I spit out, "Who the hell do you think you are?"

"I think the question is who are you? I'm pretty open about my identity."

"Do you think I've gone to the lengths I have to disguise myself for grins and giggles?" By now, I've given up all attempts to disguise my voice. Not only am I making no effort to mask it, but it has risen several decibels.

"Do you think I enjoy dressing in the most unflattering costumes I can find?" My breathing coming hard and heavy, I lean in. "Do you think I enjoy being made fun of or, worse yet, looked through? Scraping my hair back so tight it gives me a headache? Wearing god-awful glasses I can barely see through?

"Who do you think you are, invading my privacy? Kissing me whenever you feel like it? Do you do that with every girl you spend time with? And what was that fight about today? All you did is draw attention to me. Stars save me from hormonal boys." By now I'm really wound up.

Halfway through my rant, I've wiped the smile right off his face. He asks quietly, "Why do you wear a disguise?"

"It's none of your damn business." I stalk past him and head up the trail, fuming. The sound of a kicked pebble alerts me. I whirl, sliding a bit on the sandy trail. He reaches out to help me. I swat his hand away. "What are you doing?"

"I said I'd teach you to kick Fahrenbacher's ass, remember?"

"Right now I'd rather kick yours."

"Uh, yeah, I got that impression. I'll show you how it's done, then you can have a go at me."

I study him, considering. The idea holds appeal. "All right, you're on."

His smile comes perilously close to being a smirk, but he's smart enough not to crow over having won. I grab a branch and hoist myself up along the trail, Tyler still at my heels.

We reach the top of the trail and walk in the back door of the little bungalow. "Gramps," I call out.

"In the kitchen, hon," he yells back.

I stalk to the kitchen, Tyler close behind me. "We've got company."

Gramps turns around.

"Hello, Mr. Dunn."

Gramps takes in Tyler's appearance with commendable calm. "Tyler." He nods before raising his eyebrows at me.

I shake my head.

"I was just about to fix some burgers, care to join us?"

I close my eyes and bite back a groan.

Tyler looks at me. "Piper?"

"Do whatever you want," I snap, pulling plates out of the cabinet. He will anyway.

"Don't mind my granddaughter. She gets testy when she's hungry."

Tyler laughs. "I came over to teach her some self-defense moves. Do you mind, Mr. Dunn?"

Gramps pauses, his hands on the cast iron skillet. He straightens. "Does she need them?"

"It's always a good idea to know how to defend one's self."

"Don't be a politician, boy. Does she need them?"

"Fahrenbacher's been giving her grief. I can handle him when I'm around, but I'd like to know she can take care of herself when I'm not."

Gramps nods.

"Would you two stop talking about me like I'm not here?" I clench my jaw in frustration. "He fought Fahrenbacher today." I give Tyler an evil look. "You have no more sense than a gnat. You nearly drowned. You can't be completely recovered."

Gramps ignores my tirade and turns to Tyler. "Did you win?"

"Yeah."

"Good." He turns back to the stove.

"I don't believe this." I throw my hands in the air.

"Dinner'll be ready in twenty minutes."

"I can show you some basic moves in that time," Tyler tells me.

Gramps turns back. "What kind of moves you got in mind, boy?" Though his voice is gruff, there's a twinkle in his eyes.

Heat floods my face. "Gramps!"

Tyler clears his throat. "Self-defense, sir."

"Good. Go. Go." He waves his spatula at us before turning back to the stove.

"Give me two minutes to throw on sweats." I race down the hall, pull on sweats and a tee, and am back, if not in two minutes, under five.

We walk outside. There's a clear spot filled with soft thick grass just past the patio. The sky has turned to a violet that will darken to rich ebony in another few hours. Stars make their appearance. The patio light throws a soft yellow glow on the grass where we stand.

He moves toward me, his arms outstretched. My heart thumping, I swat them away. "Keep your hands to yourself."

He laughs, a sound singularly Tyler, rich and full of life. "That makes teaching self-defense a bit of a challenge."

"You'll manage," I say shortly.

He starts to circle me. I circle with him.

"If you think you can outrun someone, do it. If not, use the element of surprise." He continues to circle me. "Don't be the victim, be the aggressor. You're not going to take any shit from me."

I grin.

He doesn't. "Give me some attitude. Move in and slap your hands over my ears."

I remember him doing the same thing to Fahrenbacher. I step in and clap him smartly against the head, both hands over his ears. He winces and nods. "That's it. But if someone had been attacking you for real, you'd need to put all your strength into it."

"You didn't with Fahrenbacher."

He gives me a surprised look. "Was it obvious?"

"You held back."

"I wanted to sting him, not break his eardrums."

"But I want to?" We continue to circle each other.

"If someone comes at you intending to hurt you, you hurt them first, especially if it's a guy that's got weight and muscle on his side."

I nod.

He grabs my shoulders.

"Hey, I said no touching." I squirm but his grip only tightens.

"Do something about it."

I lift my knee but he jumps back without letting go of my shoulders. From there he moves his hands to the back of my neck. "Okay, now fist your hands together, put them inside my arms, and push up."

I clench my hands and thrust up. Surprise surges through me when his arms fall away. I chortle gleefully. "Let's do that again." I like this one.

"Fine. Only this time, after you break my grasp, clap my ears."

"Don't worry, I'll be gentle."

He snorts.

We circle and practice the two moves he's shown me.

"Dinner's ready." Gramps stands in the doorway. I don't know how long he's been watching.

We drop our arms.

"That's great. I'm starved." Tyler pushes his hair back from his forehead.

To my embarrassment, my stomach rumbles in agreement.

Tyler chuckles.

Gramps heads back to the kitchen with Tyler and me at his heels.

"I need to wash up." Tyler states the obvious. I point to the little bathroom down the hall and go to my bathroom to do the same. By the time I get to the kitchen, Tyler has made himself at home, putting ice in the glasses, and pouring iced tea.

I hold my stomach in to keep it from rumbling. Gramps puts a basket of fries on the table and a plate of burgers. I get the condiments.

We sit down and dive in. I saturate a fry in ketchup, pop it in my mouth, and glance at Tyler. He smiles at me, the burger inches away from those luscious lips. His eyes widen. The burger plops back onto his plate.

"What's wrong?" I lean forward.

Gramps' forehead wrinkles, his expression concerned. "You okay, boy?"

Tyler gives a weak smile. "I'm a goner."

"Excuse me?" I half-rise to my feet intending to feel his forehead. He's looked flushed all evening.

He motions me back and shakes his head, his voice bemused. "Between that voice and those eyes, I don't stand a chance."

Gramps harrumphs into his napkin.

I roll my eyes. "Oh, please."

"Your geek look is to keep us poor saps away," he says with conviction.

I glance at Gramps. His lips twitch. He shoves a huge bite of burger in his mouth, but his eyes continue to twinkle. A piece of melted cheese plops on his plate, distracting me.

"Yeah, that's right." I take a gulp of iced tea. Not that I need my system jump-started more than it already is.

"Where did you learn your self-defense moves, Tyler?" Gramps tries for a little diplomacy.

"My cousins." Tyler picks up his burger again and this time manages to get it between his teeth.

"Not from around here are they? I haven't heard of any other Carlisle or Carlisle kin in these parts." Gramps has polished off his burger and is working on his fries.

"Nope. Chicago."

"That explains the self-defense." Gramps grunts.

Tyler nods. He chews on his burger and studies me. "Gonna tell me about those eyes and that siren's voice?" He gives me that quick quirky grin. "I could listen to it forever."

"It does sound like angels singing," Gramps adds softly.

"Well?" Tyler cocks his head and looks at me.

"No." I toss my napkin on the table. My stomach feels queasy. I've no idea whether it's the grease or the question.

Tyler opens his mouth, no doubt to protest, but before he has an opportunity, Gramps says, "Son."

"Yes, sir." Tyler turns his attention to Gramps.

"You're young, but I can tell you've been raised a gentleman. A gentleman doesn't push if a lady isn't of a mind to share her secrets. He also keeps his lips closed about what he knows of her." His gaze holds Tyler's.

"You don't need to worry about that, sir. I'd never break a trust."

"Didn't think you would." Ice cubes clink against glass as Gramps picks up his iced tea and drinks.

Tyler turns his attention to me. "You're an excellent swimmer."

I take that to be Tyler's attempt at noncontroversial conversation. Thanks to Gramps, I've dodged another bullet. I look at him calmly eating his supper, his hands perfectly clean but gnarled with the beginning of arthritis. A rush of love overwhelms me. What would I do without him?

Tyler clears his throat, waiting.

I focus my attention back on him. For an instant, I forget to breathe, lost in the clear blue of his eyes. Everything else recedes into the background, even Gramps. His gaze, holding mine, grows intense. I can swear heat rises from the table.

Gramps clears his throat. "Would someone pass the salt?"

My breath goes out in a whoosh. I feel somewhat better when Tyler blinks. He looks as bemused as I feel.

Gramps mutters, "Young'uns," and shakes his head.

I pass the salt before turning my attention back to Tyler. "Tell me about your cousins."

He leans back against the chair, balancing it on two legs and gives me a speculative look before smiling in a manner that causes demons to dance in his eyes. "We have some secrets of our own in my family. When you're ready to exchange family skeletons, let me know. I've got stories that will curl your hair. I'll tell you mine when you tell me yours."

He cuts my gramps a look and holds up his hand. "I'm not pushing."

Gramps grunts.

I shake my head, push back the chair, and start stacking the dishes. Tyler rises, gathers his, and heads for the sink. "I hate to eat and run, but I better head home."

"Not a problem. Where'd you park?"

"About a half mile down the beach."

I tuck in my chin and give him the look. It's so obvious he came to spy on me.

He shrugs without any apparent guilt. "Want to walk me to my car?" He grins. "I'll drive you back."

Indecisive, I bite my lip.

"Go ahead, Pip. I'll load the dishwasher."

I really have doubts about this. Self-defense and dinner with Gramps is one thing, but walking with Tyler on the beach, under the stars? That's a different kettle of fish. "Okay."

"Are you ready?" I turn to Tyler.

"In a moment." He steps up to Gramps and holds out his hand. "I never thanked you, sir, for saving my life. I'm in your debt."

Gramps takes his hand and looks him in the eye. "I'm not the one who saved you. Nor am I the one you owe a debt to. Don't forget it."

"Yes, sir. I won't, sir."

Gramps nods, moves to the counter and begins to load the dishes.

We walk out the back door. Tyler unwraps a couple of peppermints, hands me one and takes one himself. The bite of mint fills my mouth and cools my tongue. Heading for the path, I look longingly at the edge of the cliff. Diving would be much quicker. I suck it up. Sometimes one has to make sacrifices for the cause.

Tyler follows me cautiously. Luckily, the bright moon and stars light the path.

"He's an awesome ole dude, even if he is a bit intimidating."

"Don't call him old," I snap.

"Ole, Piper. Not old. You aren't planning on majoring in English are you?"

"They mean the same, goof."

"Oh well, I'm not planning on being an English major either."

I can hear the grin in his voice. I shake my head.

"Let me guess. You're leaning toward science."

"Yeah, so?"

When we reach the bottom of the trail, he takes my hand. I tug but he doesn't let go. Oh, what the heck. I enjoy the novel sensation of a boy's warm hand wrapped around mine, especially this boy.

He swings my hand back and forth as we walk the beach in companionable silence. The melodic call of "ka-ty-did, ka-ty-did" sounds nearby from an orchestra of crickets, the measured cadence of the ocean in the background.

We round the bend, leaving my private beach for the public one. Up ahead, I see Tyler's black SUV parked alongside the road.

"Help!"

I whip around. A hand pops out of the water, followed by a head. "Help," the swimmer yells again.

Still wearing my swimsuit, I strip off my sweats and run into the shallows, Tyler at my heels. I dive into the water and head toward the swimmer. When I get close, I see it's a young man. I reach him quickly. He isn't that far out, but he's hit a deep pocket. I swim up behind him and grab him around the shoulders, trying to avoid his flailing arms. I manage until one of his hands pops me in the eye.

"Oww. Damn it." I tighten my grip. "Calm down. I've got you. I won't let you drown." I talk in my normal voice, hoping to quiet him. He immediately stops fighting and lets me tow him.

"Can't swim. Waded out too far," he gasps, kicking out with his feet, trying to help me.

"You must have just gone under," I observe.

"Yeah, it just happened. Glad you heard me."

I frown. His voice sounds familiar, but I can't worry about that now.

Tyler reaches my other side, smart enough to keep his distance and stay out of my way. In minutes, we've reached the shore.

"What the hell happened, Rick?" Tyler asks as we stagger out of the water.

As I let go of him I take a good look at my rescue victim. *Holy freaking crap.* It's all I can do not to put my head in my hands and moan. The boy I've rescued is Rick Sabatini from my social studies class.

Chapter 12

"Thank you." He coughs and leans against me, shaking.

What do I do now? I stand paralyzed, my body rigid. Lucky for me, Tyler thinks on his feet. He puts his arm around Rick and propels him to the dirt road where Rick's car is parked.

Rick's raspy voice carries back to me as I try to blend with the shadows. "What are you doing here? You didn't even give me a chance to thank her."

Tyler keeps walking, towing Rick with him.

"What a goddess. Do you know her? Who is she?"

I nearly collapse with relief. He doesn't recognize me. My hearing is particularly acute, better in the water, but I do just fine on land, so I can hear the entire embarrassing conversation. I lean forward and tip my head, anxious to hear Tyler's reply.

"That's information I'm not prepared to share with you, bro."

"Man you have all the luck. Every girl in Rosemont is after you and you manage to find the most spectacular piece of ass on the planet. Maybe she's a sea siren. She has the voice of an angel."

At this point, I put my head in my hands and groan.

"Let me remind you, that spectacular piece of ass just saved your life." Tyler's voice has an edge to it.

"You're right. I'm sorry. I'm not myself. I nearly drowned."

"Yeah, you did. So be more respectful."

"You're right. I should go back and thank her."

"Never mind, I'll thank her for you. Do you have your keys?"

The shadowy figure feels his pockets. I hear a ripping sound.

He says in a relieved voice, "Thank God for Velcro."

"You okay to drive?" Tyler opens Rick's door without waiting for an answer.

"I'm fine."

"Good. See you tomorrow."

"Yeah, see ya." His engine purrs to life.

I step further back into the shadows so his headlights won't pick me up when he turns the car around.

Tyler walks toward me. The moon limns his features, casting shadows beneath the high cheek bones, outlining his nose—that is just the least bit crooked—and lighting his lips. He stops in front of me.

"How can he not see you?" he marvels.

"I'd say he saw me just fine." I tear my gaze away from those perfect lips. They aren't too thin or too full, kissable.

He grins. His eyes twinkle. Or maybe it's the stars reflected in them. "Oh, well, to paraphrase Rick. You do have a fine ass."

I grimace, somewhat pleased, somewhat embarrassed.

He steps nearer, his mouth so close his breath warms my face, and the fresh scent of peppermint zings my senses.

"I guess it's official, Rick says we're dating." He lays his hands lightly on my shoulders.

"That's not exactly what he said. Plus I've never had the desire to join a harem." I snort and start to pull back. His warm hands settle more firmly on my shoulders.

"My prowess with the opposite sex is somewhat overrated." He pulls me closer. "I have no problems with monogamy."

My heart does a slow hard thud. I want to tap my ear to see if I'm hearing right. Instead, I force myself to pull away. "I need to get home."

He lets me go, grabs my hand, and walks toward his car. "Didn't your mother ever warn you men like nothing better than a challenge?"

"Oh please." I roll my eyes.

He chuckles and opens the car door. I hesitate.

"What?" he asks.

"I don't want to ruin your seats."

"You won't. To an extent leather is waterproof. I'll wipe off any excess when I get home. Cleaning car seats 101: you can clean mildew off leather with an equal ratio of water and alcohol."

"Too much information." I slide in and lean back against the smooth seat. It smells of sand, sea salt, and Tyler.

"Your Gramps would appreciate the info even if you don't. Actually, he probably already knows." He walks around and climbs in the driver's side. In moments, we're heading up the dirt road that leads to Gramps' cottage.

Tyler pulls up to the cottage and shuts off the motor.

                   Sandra Cox

"You don't have to see me to the door." I reach for the handle but before I can open the door, Tyler pulls me to him. "You're my girl." His voice still has a thread of laughter.

"I'm…" Before I can say any more, his lips settle warm and persuasive on mine. It certainly feels like I'm his girl. When he finally releases me, I sit, blinking at him. He leans across me and opens the door. "Sleep well." He gives me a light kiss on the tip of my nose.

I stumble out of the car. The wind on my face revives me and brings reality rushing back. Jeez what am I thinking? Once again, my feelings for this boy have gotten the best of me. More perturbed with myself than him—after all he's only a guy—I huff, "I'm not anyone's girl." I slam the door with more force than necessary.

"You can run all you want, sea girl, but one of these days you're going to admit it." The words and the certainty of his voice follow me into the cottage.

Chapter 13

Another sleepless night. I wake heavy-lidded and out of sorts, though Gramps' hotcakes and the steaming mug of coffee he sticks under my noise go a long way to bringing me around before I head for classes.

The morning is uneventful. I manage to avoid both twins, which is nothing short of a miracle. They're extremely tenacious where I'm concerned.

As usual, I'm running late for Mr. Grumble's class. I can't work up any energy for calculus. I hurry in. *Crap*. The only empty seat is between Holly and Tyler. I plop my hiney in it as the bell rings and look straight ahead, determined not to draw more attention to myself than possible. Seated between the twins, I should know that's impossible.

"Hey, gorgeous," Tyler whispers.

I ignore the flutter in my tummy, scowl, and don't respond. It's only one hour, then Tyler will be in a different class. Papers shuffle, Grumble drones on, making mind-numbing equations on the board. Supposedly, next year the students will get iPads and work equations on tablets, but cutting-edge technology is still in the talking stage at Rosemont. My eyes grow heavy. I begin to nod.

I get elbows in both ribs at the same time. I straighten. Geez, what is it with twins anyway? Heat rises in my cheeks as I think of Tyler's kisses. I hope Holly isn't psychic.

When the bell finally rings, I stagger to my feet in need of more caffeine. The twins rise with me. I nod at the right moments as Holly chatters about clothes and hair. When we turn right to go to social studies, Tyler turns with us. I stop. My muscles tighten and I bite my lip. "Your class is in the other direction."

"Yeah, I'll get there in time. I thought I'd walk you girls to Soc."

"I'd rather you didn't." My jaw tight, I clutch my book bag to my chest. Rick Sabatini is in this class. It's the reason I didn't get any sleep last night. The last thing I want is for him to see me with Tyler.

The twinkle in Tyler's eyes dims. "All right. See you later."

Not if I can help it. I like the boy, but I'm a big believer in survival. Why can't he leave me alone?

Holly looks back and forth between us, her eyes wide, her brows raised. I watch Tyler's loose, lanky stride as he walks away. I feel a moment's regret. I feel safer when he's around, less exposed, which is really an oxymoron because my exposure shoots through the roof around him.

A guy and girl wave as they walk by, demonstrating my point.

Holly tugs me down the hall. "Okay, what's going on? Give."

"What do you mean?" I try to play dumb but Holly is having none of it.

"Okay, you saved his life this weekend, for which I'm eternally grateful. Have I thanked you yet?"

"Only about a thousand times." I grin in spite of myself. Holly has that effect.

"Then, he spends all kinds of time at your house. And this morning I hear him tell Josie McAllister—when she asks if he'd like to catch a movie—he's in a relationship."

I stop. Students flow around me like water. One girl jostles my elbow, mumbles an apology, and keeps going. Holly tugs my arm. I start moving again. My head reels. Everything looks like rainbow bursts. The cylindrical lighting fixtures give off warm spurts of sunlight. All is right with the world…for about ten seconds. Reality crashes in. This is exactly what I don't need.

"Really?"

Holly gives a snort of exasperation. "Come on, don't hold back. When did you and my brother become an item?"

"What are you talking about?" I beat back the heat rising in my cheeks, hoping it's partially hidden by the glasses, and lift my chin. I give her an incredulous look. At least, that's what I'm shooting for. I don't doubt for a moment, these hideous glasses hide my facial expression, except perhaps for my mouth that's puckered like a prune.

"Piper, what's your GPA?"

"Say what?"

"What is your GPA?" she repeats in patient tones.

"Have you lost your mind?" I demand, excusing myself as I bounce off a thin boy headed in the opposite direction.

"Answer the question."

"Four point, if you must know." It's the dolphin DNA. They're extremely intelligent creatures. "What's yours?"

"Three point nine. But this has got nothing to do with me."

"Why are we talking about GPA?" I admit I'm confused.

"The point is you're too smart to think I'd fall for that 'it's got nothing to do with me' routine." She hoists her book bag, which is sliding off her shoulder.

"Your brother and I are not an item." I keep my eyes straight ahead. At least the conversation has taken my mind off the upcoming confrontation.

Rick Sabatini is sitting in the front row closest to the door. He stands up as I walk in.

Chapter 14

My heart thunders. My legs feel like lead. It's all I can do to keep moving.

Sensing my tension, Holly throws me a bewildered look. I shake my head.

"Hey, Holly." Rick comes over to us.

"Hi, Rick." Holly smiles.

"I was wondering if you'd like to go a party Friday night."

The tension in my neck and shoulders loosens fractionally.

"Sure that would be fun."

He turns to me. I tense. "Piper."

"Rick."

"So Tyler and Fahrenbacher got in a dust-up over you, huh?"

I swallow. "Yeah, my beauty drives guys wild."

He laughs as I intend. "Speaking of beauties." He turns his attention back to Holly. "Your brother was with one of the most incredible girls I've ever seen, yourself excluded of course," he throws in hastily.

"Oh really?" Holly quivers like a pointer after a rabbit.

"Yeah, she saved my life. I would have drowned if she hadn't swum out and rescued me."

The bell rings. Never in my life have I been so glad to hear that obnoxious sound. I nudge Holly and make my way to two seats open in the back.

Holly says goodbye to Rick and follows me.

With a rustle of book bags, we slide into our seats, Holly murmuring greetings all around her. She leans toward me and speaks softly so only I can hear. "My, my, two lives in less than a week. You have been busy."

Holy freaking crap.

"I don't know what you're talking about."

"Of course, you don't."

I open my mouth.

"Ms. Dunn, tell us the pros and cons of gun control."

I blink. Until that moment, I've never believed in divine intervention. I'll have to rethink that one. Thank you, Mrs. Wilson. I expound on the subject till Mrs. Wilson's eyes glaze over and I hear several yawns.

"Uh, yes, thank you, Miss Dunn," Mrs. Wilson finally cuts me off and moves on to another student less longwinded on the subject.

Finally, the bell rings. I scoop up my books and hurry out of the classroom. Unfortunately, Holly's on my heels. "I knew it. I knew you were a beauty under those dowdy clothes," Holly crows, her legs pumping to keep up with me.

One of the basketball players passes us. Shaking his head, he snorts in disbelief.

"Shut up, Holly." My lips clench.

"Sorry. It's top secret, huh?"

"Just drop it."

I hurry into my physics class. A seat at the front of the room catches my eye. I head for it, leaving Holly to fend for herself. For a moment, I put my head in my hands. I want to howl. My world is unraveling and all because I can't keep the twins at bay.

I did just fine before they came to town. No one paid any attention to Piper the geek. What if Rick had made the connection? I shudder then straighten. He didn't. My disguise is intact. No one expects anything but what they see. I will just have to find a way to discourage the twins without hurting their feelings.

On that self-righteous note, I turn my attention to the lecture. I manage to stay focused till the bell rings. When it does, I hop up and make a beeline for the door. Lucky for me, several of Holly's admirers and friends cluster around her. I make my escape.

Physics is my last class. I manage to avoid Holly and Tyler as I head for my truck. I should be happy I've succeeded. Instead, I feel something I normally keep at bay, loneliness. I hurry home with no Carlisle twins to stop me. They're probably headed for the Cat and lattes, surrounded by admirers.

I grimace and clutch the steering wheel harder than necessary. Sucking air, I lean back and force myself to relax. So Tyler told Josie he was in a relationship. I glance in the rearview mirror and catch the goofy grin on my face. I wipe it off. I'll have to set the boy straight. I push on the gas. Beulah groans and chugs up the hill, white exhaust pouring from her tailpipe.

I kill the motor and run into the house, the screen door banging shut behind me.

"Gramps?"

No answer. I trot to my room, toss my book bag on the bed, and strip out of my geeky clothes. I pull the pins out of my hair and shake it. I pull boxers over my white and gold two-piece. Whew. Now that I've shed the geek attire, I feel more myself. I plop down at my computer determined to get some homework done. An hour later, I head for the kitchen intent on fixing dinner. Smells coming from a cardboard box sitting on the table tickle my nostrils.

"Pizza. Way to go, Gramps." My stomach rumbles about the same time my mouth starts watering.

He chuckles. Ice rattles as he places two glasses of Coke on the table. We sit down and dive in.

"Tyler coming over tonight?" He bites into a steaming piece of pie.

"Nope."

He chews and swallows. "Everything all right there?"

"There's nothing to be all right or otherwise."

"Honey, that boy likes you."

With a sigh, I set it back down. "You know I can't get into a relationship."

"I don't want you being alone."

"I'm not alone. I've got you." I smile at him.

He doesn't smile back. He looks troubled. "I'm not getting any younger. I won't be around forever."

"Don't say that." I clamp my lips together. I can't think of Gramps not being around.

"Don't worry about it, honey. I didn't mean to upset you."

"Are you feeling okay?" I tip my head and study him, frowning. He's mentioned his mortality several times lately. Is there a reason for it?

"I'm fine. Just trying to be practical."

"Well, stop it. I don't like practical." I reach over and squeeze his hand.

He squeezes back. I let go and reach for the pizza. To my surprise it's all gone.

"I'm going swimming." Before I can rise, a knock sounds at the door.

"I wonder who that is."

"I wonder," Gramps echoes somewhat sarcastically.

I shake my head and hurry to the door. "Tyler." I'm genuinely surprised.

"Ready for your self-defense lesson?" His voice is constrained, his face sober.

Gramps comes up behind me. "Hi, Tyler."

"Hi, Mr. Dunn." His greeting to Gramps is much warmer than the one he's given me.

I sigh. I'm so not used to dealing with the fragile ego of a male.

"Won't you come in?" Gramps invites.

"Thanks, but I'm just here for Piper's self-defense lesson."

"Right." Gramps nods.

"I didn't realize you were coming over." I walk outside and fall into step beside him.

"Would you rather I hadn't?" Not waiting for an answer he continues, "Whether you want to see me or not you need to learn self-defense."

"I appreciate you taking the time to show me. Did you guys go to the Cat after school?"

Without answering, he moves to the car and reaches in the open window. I raise my eyebrows, curious. He turns and hands me an iced latte.

Before I can control my response, I give him a megawatt smile and say spontaneously, "Oh, Tyler, how thoughtful."

He thaws visibly.

I take a sip of the chocolaty caffeine. "Perfect."

He rocks back on his heels his hands in his back pockets. "Why didn't you want me walking you to class today?"

"Because Rick Sabatini is in that class and I'm afraid if he sees us together he might make the connection."

"Oh." His breath whooshes out. "I thought you didn't want to be with me."

"It's not that I don't want to be with you. It's just not a good idea." I run a finger around the condensation on the outside of the glass.

"Why, Piper? Why isn't it a good idea?" He stands close to me, his expression intense, his eyes lit with passionate inquiry. Tension pours off him in waves.

"Because you're the most popular boy in school and I'm trying to keep a low profile."

"I don't get it. Other than driving all the boys at school wild, why would you want to hide behind those glasses and clothes? Not that I mind," he adds hastily. "After seeing Rick salivate all over you, I like your wardrobe better all the time." He grins. Crinkles deepen around his mouth and eyes.

"You don't need to know that." My body stiff, I wait for his anger at what he could consider rejection.

He surprises me. "Fair enough. Just remember, you're my girl." He winks at me. On his face is the expression of supreme confidence only the male of the species has mastered.

"I am so not your girl." My teeth grind together. How can he be so stubborn?

He swoops in. His warm peppermint breath lingers on my face for a moment before his lips find mine. My world tilts. Is it like this with any boy? I can't imagine my reaction being the same with anyone else.

His arms pull me close. His hands slide around my waist. He pulls me against him, his hard body pressed against mine.

I throw my arms around him and return the pressure of his lips, my tongue sliding between his teeth. My blood races in a wash of heat through my system. My core melts.

The kiss goes on and on.

Reluctantly, he pushes me away. He gives me a crooked grin, his breath coming hard and fast. I put my hand against his heart and feel it thunder beneath my palm. I stare at him dazed, my world still spinning.

"And you say you're not my girl," he whispers, his lips twitching.

Still on fire, my brain stalled, I can't form a reply.

"I came to give you another self-defense lesson, but I don't think having my hands on you is a good idea. I think I'll go home and take a cold shower instead." He grins and shakes his head. "See you tomorrow." Unable to speak, I nod.

He turns and walks away.

The idea of a cold shower holds appeal. I strip down to my bathing suit, walk down the path to the cliff edge, and dive. Cool blue water closes around me. I blow bubbles under water and push forward, kicking with my feet.

The fog surrounding my brain lifts, replaced by a thought that fills me with pure terror. What if Gramps was watching?

The bubbles coming from my mouth increase when I groan. How could a simple kiss make me lose contact with reality? Although on reflection, there's nothing simple about Tyler's kisses. Or about the boy himself.

A pink and purple sheephead swims under my nose, distracting me. It's one of nature's fascinating anomalies that starts life as a female and ends as a male. Me, I'm pretty sure I want to remain a female. I smile. Oh yeah, there are definite perks.

A shadow darkens the water just before I'm bumped, hard.

Chapter 15

Mouth open, I swallow water. Trying not to choke, I kick to the surface and chuff. The sun has set. Moonlight glistens on lazy waves like a thousand sparkling diamonds. Dog paddling, I pull my hair away from my face and wring it out.

Something cold and smooth smacks against my body, again. I turn in a circle, looking for the intruder. A few yards away, a dolphin's head pops up. It starts to chatter, the sound sharp and staticky. This dolphin isn't interested in play.

She dives out of sight before coming up a few yards away, chattering again. This time more high-pitched and squeaky. Again she dives down and breaks the surface farther away, still chattering.

I start toward her. She looks at me, as if to make sure I'm following, before heading out to sea. We swim about a mile before she stops. In the distance, an engine hums and the lights of an approaching vessel cut through the gloom. Cautiously, I swim forward to get a better look. A chill that has nothing to do with the cool water runs the length of my body.

Oh my God! Fear paralyzes me. I stare in disbelief. The ship has a mobile platform. What is a research vessel doing this close to my home?

The dolphin splashes her tail in the water to get my attention before diving down. I follow, my limbs stiff, my movements jerky. The dolphin stops swimming and floats. I pull alongside her.

My heart beats fast and hard, thumping against my rib cage. Up ahead is a sophisticated marine mammal trap, a young dolphin captured inside. The dolphin is around the same size as the one I played with the other day. I swim forward to study it.

A bait bucket of finely woven mesh houses a hundred small fish. It's what lured the young dolphin in. The trap sprung when contact was made with the mesh bucket.

The baby cries pitifully. Its mother answers. There's no room for it to turn around.

I study the trap. It would be a simple matter to slash the mesh. I reach for my knife. My heart sinks. Lately, I've been in too much of a hurry to strap it on, a dangerous mistake. I swim closer and study the mouth of the trap. I'll have to figure out how to spring it.

I run my hands around the round lip and find a hinge. Now, all I have to do is find the spring. Painstakingly, I run my hands along the cool metal.

The baby continues to cry. His mom bumps her snout against the wire mesh near his head to comfort him.

I run my hands around the frame twice before I discover it. My chest heaving, I breathe a sigh of relief. I press the spring.

Nothing happens.

Mom starts to chatter at me, the sound sharp and high-pitched. Both she and the baby are nervous.

Even in the cold water, beads of sweat form on my body.

This time when I press on the spring and stick my fingers inside the mesh, I pull against the frame. It gives an inch and snaps back into place.

Encouraged, I try again. I grunt, pushing the lever and pulling at the edge of the frame. I manage to get it open a couple of inches. I pause when I hear a whirring noise.

The ropes tighten and the trap begins to move upward.

Chapter 16

Panic hits. *Crap.* I've got to get the baby out and I've run out of time.

Bracing my feet against the other side of the trap, I push hard on the hinge and pull on the frame with all my might. What if I can't get it open? Frantic, I run my hands up and down the container. My fingers find another small spring I've overlooked. I push on both springs at the same time and the door swings wide, with me hanging on it.

The pulley is moving faster through the water. Above, I can see the surface. The baby darts out. My fingers are stiff. I have to pry them open. Finally, I disentangle them from the door and let my body sink into the depths.

Two shadowy figures lean over the side. Their muffled voices drift down. "I was sure we'd caught one."

"What the hell?" The other voice becomes more indistinct as I continue downward. "The trap's been sprung!"

I glance up and see the blurry outline of two men hanging over the edge of the boat staring into the sea. I know I'm too far down for them to see. Even so, I'm not planning on hanging around. I stop drifting and swim away from the ship.

The two dolphins flashed out of sight as soon as the baby was free. Water ripples around me as mom and baby come back. They swim on each side of me. The baby noses me with its snout. The mother chatters beside me. I put my hands on their fins and float. Squeaking, they pull me along. I blow bubbles, my body going limp as I glide, the water rippling along my spine.

I let go of the fins, grab my knees, and flip over and over like a ball. Chattering, the dolphins flip too. Euphoric at freeing the baby and escaping a close call, I play with them a while longer before I surface out of sight of the vessel. I head home, the moon lighting a path on the water.

When I get to the cottage, I find Gramps sitting in his favorite chair, a pipe clamped in his teeth, watching the news.

"Went to the ocean, huh? I thought you were going to do self-defense." He rattles the paper, his voice mild, never looking up.

I beat back the heat rising in my cheeks. The research vessel and the trapped dolphin drove Tyler and his kisses right out of my mind, which goes to show how upset I was. "He left and I went for a swim."

Gramps lowers the paper. "Tyler seems like a responsible young man, but still and all he's a young man."

"Oh, Gramps, not the birds and the bees." I squirm, shifting from one foot to the other. This conversation could be worse than being tossed into an experimental lab.

"I'm not talking birds and bees, I'm talking horn dogs."

Oh yeah, definitely worse. "Ewww." I scrunch up my nose, totally mortified. Surely, Gramps is too old to remember birds, bees, and horn dogs.

"Something weird happened in the ocean tonight, Gramps." If it hadn't I would have invented something, I'm that desperate to change the subject.

I slide down on the couch and clutch a worn blue throw pillow to my middle.

"Oh?" Gramps raises his eyebrows. A small smile crinkles his features. He knows I'm changing the subject.

"It was strange. Several miles out there was a research vessel."

Gramps straightens. A frown creases his forehead.

"They'd set a trap. There was a young dolphin caught in it." I clutch my pillow tighter. Speaking of it brings back the abject terror of the moment. I start to shake.

"Catching the dolphin could have been an accident." He knocks the ashes into the old brown ceramic ashtray at his elbow.

I take deep breaths. The shaking subsides. I trust Gramps didn't notice. "I'm counting on it." My temple throbs. I rub it and ask what has been on my mind since the incident, "You don't think they could be working for the agency that grafted my mother do you? The one that 'created' her to help plant bombs on ships and find underwater mines?" Bile rises in my throat, bitter as my thoughts. A human who could swim like a dolphin. I take a deep breath and shake off the harsh memories. No time for that now. Gramps runs his hand across his chin causing a light rasping sound. He looks at me, his expression troubled. "I don't know. But I'd say you made the right decision not sharing your secret with young Tyler."

"Yeah." My shoulders slump.

Gramps reaches over and pats me awkwardly. "Don't worry about it. You're safe. They couldn't possibly know about you."

I give him a small smile. "I know." I push up from the couch. "I'm going to finish my homework." I kiss him on top of his head, pit stop by the kitchen to grab a glass of milk and a bag of chips and head for my room. Three hours later, I fall into bed, determined to forget the whole, petrifying incident. Unfortunately, my subconscious has other ideas. I spend the night dreaming about being strapped to a table where my body is dissected into little pieces and replaced with dolphin parts, while the baby dolphin looks on crying.

The next thing I know the alarm clock's blasting. *Thank God.* I fumble with the button and the screeching stops. "Another wonderful day at Rosemont." Actually, it looks pretty good after the night I spent.

I take a deep breath and compartmentalize last night to the far corner of my mind. I can't deal with it right now. For an instant, I wonder what it would feel like to throw off my disguise and do the normal things young women my age do. Giggle with a group of girls and talk about boys over lattes. And have a steady boyfriend.

I reach for the end of my ribbed cami to pull it over my head. My hands shake. So much for compartmentalizing, I drop my hands and gaze out the window and think of something more pleasant than captured dolphins and dolph-girls. The sun winks at me. A small wren tweets a greeting. "I like Tyler, a lot," I tell the bird.

He sings back at me.

"Yeah, you're right. This is my life. I need to deal with it and put away silly dreams. He's human. I'm a dolph-girl. A dolph-girl who could end up in a cage with her dolphin buddies." Still, when I get dressed, I use a light fragrant perfume and add some turquoise earrings. I look in the mirror. "Geek with earrings." Dissatisfied with my appearance, I shrug and leave the haven of my room.

I breakfast with Gramps and head out.

A group of boys and girls lounge against the worn red brick exterior a few yards from the doors. The sun sparkles on the silver letters that spell out Rosemont High School. Tyler steps out of the group and toward me. My heart does a flip of welcome before I crease my forehead into a frown.

"Good morning, sunshine." He steps closer. The smell of soap and a spicy aftershave tickles my senses and makes my mouth water. I scowl harder.

He grins. "Okay, maybe I should revise that to cloudshine."

I snort. "What do you want, Tyler?"

Sandra Cox

He steps closer and gives a theatrical sigh. "I can tell I've been way too subtle. I want you, Piper Dunn."

Heat rises then pools in the lower part of my stomach. I'm eighteen and my hormones are in overdrive. For a second, I romanticize.

Reality sets in. How much will he want me once he discovers my blowhole? 'Oh, baby, your blowhole makes me hot.' Yeah right. I shake myself free of fantasies. "I suggest you look to your cheerleaders. I don't sleep around."

"Geez that's bitchy."

"You think?" I shove past him and head toward the double doors.

I sigh as he opens one for me.

"Though, I am glad you don't sleep around," he continues, hoisting his book bag into a more comfortable position across his shoulders.

I ignore him and stride determinedly forward.

He keeps pace easily. "Nice earrings," is his next gambit. "I don't think I've ever seen you wear jewelry before."

I look straight ahead and stretch out my legs. He leans in and sniffs. "Is that perfume, Ms. Dunn? Very nice. I do believe you're taking the first steps toward coming out of the closet."

I throw a quick glance at him. His eyes twinkle with deviltry.

"Go away."

"Can't."

"Can't or won't?"

"We've got the same class."

"Don't sit with me." What am I supposed to do with someone who completely refuses to take a hint?

"Since I seem to have a negative effect on your sunny disposition, I'm going to leave you alone the rest of the day. I'll be by this evening to give you self-defense lessons." He gives me a mocking grin and moves over to join the group of chattering cheerleaders throwing curious looks our way.

I fight back jealousy and reassure myself I'm relieved he left. People are starting to talk. To notice me. I grimace. Talk is an understatement. It's the number one source of endless speculation at the high school. What does the hot deee-licious Tyler Carlisle see in plain Jane Piper Dunn? Since he's seen me outside of my disguise, I know the answer to that. What I haven't figured out is why he got interested before he saw me sans disguise.

A gangly junior, with glasses and lanky black hair, who's paying as much attention to where he's going as I, bumps into me. We mutter apologies and head to our prospective classes.

Tyler's as good as his word. He doesn't approach me the entire day. Instead, he makes the bevy of senior beauties extremely happy by flirting his insufferable head off with them. At one point, he catches me watching him and winks before turning his attention to Heather Martin, the prettiest girl in school.

His twin, of course, has no such compunction and spends her time conjecturing on what I've done to cause her brother to flirt with every girl in school who has a pair of perky breasts. "He's trying to make you jealous," she decides. All in all, I'm glad when the school day ends. Wasting no time, I jump in Beulah and head home.

I beat Gramps back. Since he's been carrying the majority of the kitchen duties lately, I decide to make him meatloaf, baked potatoes, and banana pudding. His faves.

I throw a pair of pink boxers and a white tee over my hot pink two-piece then head for the kitchen. I wash the potatoes, mix the meatloaf, and pop them in the oven. While the meal cooks, I get my laptop, and feeling virtuous, get down to business at the kitchen table.

A hello sounds from the screen door I left open to catch the spring breeze. Tyler. He's earlier than I expected, though I put an extra potato on just in case.

I smooth my hair back and head for the door, unsure whether or not I should be mad about his blatant flirting. I have no claims on him and therefore nothing to be mad about. Still….

"You're early." I don't scowl when I open the screen door. I don't smile either.

"Too early?" He wears faded jeans, a white V-neck tee, and looks yummier than my banana pudding.

"Not at all. Come in."

He moves with loose-limbed grace that I find incredibly sexy. He sniffs. "Wow. Something smells good."

"Have you eaten yet?"

"No, but I wasn't angling for an invitation."

"Of course, you weren't." I give him a disbelieving look.

He laughs and throws up a hand. "Guilty. What's for supper?" He follows me in, the screen door slamming behind him.

I tell him.

"Who fixed dinner?" He wiggles his eyebrows.

"I did." I refuse to be embarrassed about it.

"So, besides your many other skills you can cook, too."

I laugh. "That may be pushing the envelope. Gramps and I both have limited dishes we know how to prepare. Meatloaf happens to be one of mine."

"Works for me."

At that moment, the screen door bangs again. "Piper?"

"In the kitchen, Gramps."

He walks in, a hardy oak bent and gnarled with age but still strong. I feel an overwhelming rush of love for him. Neither of us is overly demonstrative so instead of rushing to him and throwing my arms around him, I settle for a smile.

It's enough. He smiles back before he turns to Tyler. "Hello, Tyler. Joining us for supper?"

"If you don't mind, sir."

"You're always welcome here, son."

"Don't encourage him." I put on a mitt and pull the meatloaf out of the oven.

Gramps rubs his hands together, a look of expectant pleasure on his face when he eyes the steaming loaf of meat. Balancing the potatoes I placed in a plate in one hand and the meatloaf in the other, I order Tyler, "Make yourself useful and set the table."

"Yes, ma'am." He salutes me. I catch him winking at Gramps. I shake my head and pour the iced tea. We sit down to eat.

Gramps slits his potato. Steam rises in a sensuous wisp. "This looks wonderful."

"Thanks, Gramps." I fork in a piece of meatloaf.

"Are you young 'uns going to work on self-defense?"

"That's the plan, sir."

We chat back and forth while we eat. I can't believe how comfortable it is having Tyler spend time with Gramps and me. Almost like family.

"You two run along. I'll clean up," Gramps says when we finish.

"Thanks, Gramps."

Tyler and I walk to the backyard.

"Are you ready?" Tyler fists his hands and brings them to the sides of his face.

"Bring it on."

He jabs at me. I throw up my hands and block. "Good." He encourages before tossing a hook. I parry. We've been working about an hour when he kicks my foot out from under me. Before I fall, he grabs me and bends me over his arm. He leans in, his breath warm on my face. "Admit it."

"Admit what?" I pant, still out of breath from the workout. Tiny beads of perspiration dot my body.

He lowers his face till his lips hover above mine. "That you're my girl."

I push against him. "Don't start."

His arms tighten and his mouth claims mine. He bites gently at my bottom lip. When my mouth opens, his tongue runs across my teeth then slips inside. Heat that has nothing to do with the workout shoots through me.

His lips continue their persuasive assault. He kisses the corner of my mouth then trails kisses to my ear. "Admit you're my girl." His warm breath tickles my ear and sends a shiver through me.

I turn my head and find his mouth. Blood pounds in my ears. I grab his hair and kiss him for all I'm worth.

His heart pounds against mine. His voice hoarse, he demands, "Say it."

I shake my head, trying to clear it rather than deny his request. There's a reason this isn't a good idea, but at the moment it eludes me.

"Say it," he demands again.

"I'm your girl." In a hormonal haze, I drag his head down to mine, straining close against him. By the time we break apart, we're both panting. Tyler holds me in his arms. His warm smile washes over me. I snuggle closer, feeling as if I'm in a safe haven.

Tyler's girl. Warm bubbles of happiness fizz through me. I want to shout and dance and laugh all at the same time…before reality slaps me upside the head. I straighten. The happiness bubbles burst. What the hell have I agreed to? I glance at him through my lashes. There's no way I'm going to extinguish the light in his eyes. I've never seen Tyler vulnerable before. I give an internal sigh. We'll just have to make some compromises.

I disentangled myself. "Tyler."

"Mmm-hmm." His hands slide up and down my arms, distracting me. I try to clear my head.

"We don't need to make this public, do we?"

While the light doesn't quite go out, the bright glow notches down. He frowns, puzzled. "Why?"

Mentally, I count to ten. "I've told you on more than one occasion, I need to keep a low profile. You're at the opposite end of the spectrum." I give him a strained smile.

He grabs my hands. "True, but you haven't told me why."

"No, I haven't."

"Okay, I'll go first." He leads me to the wooden bench that sits behind the house, just out of reach of the lamplight. The sweet fragrance of a nearby lilac bush wafts over us.

The sun set nearly an hour ago. Stars bright as diamonds light the dark gray backdrop of approaching night. The moon drifts across the sky. Mother Nature must be a romantic at heart to create such a perfect setting.

"That's not necessary. Please don't." I settle back against the hard wood of the bench.

He sits down and shifts on the bench before taking my hand. "It's a matter of faith."

"Tyler…"

He interrupts. "My uncle is high up the food chain in the Chicago Mafia."

"You shouldn't—" I begin. "Say what?"

"I've never told anyone that. I've also got one that's a Navy SEAL, but that's not a secret, just a brag." He gives me a lopsided smile.

"You shouldn't have told me." My voice comes out sharper than I intend. Geez, the Mafia. This just gets better and better. I pull my hand away.

"What, that one of my uncles is a Navy SEAL?"

"You aren't that obtuse. You know perfectly well I was talking about the Mafia thing."

"Does that bother you?"

Not as much as finding out his girlfriend is a mutant would bother him. "It took me by surprise, that's all. And it's not your secret to share."

"You're right. But I wanted to prove a couple of things to you." He lets go of my hands and slides an arm around me. With the other hand, he holds up a finger ticking off points. "One, you can trust me." He holds up another finger. "And two, though it's a bad cliché, things aren't often as bad as they seem."

"Yeah right." I snort. "Not as bad as they seem." I laugh. Unfortunately, it has a hysterical edge to it.

He waits.

I take a deep breath and get myself under control. My lips clamp together, I stare at the traveling moon.

Tyler sighs. "Okay, you win. Your secret remains your secret."

"And you don't show me undue attention at school." I cock my head and lift an eyebrow.

"If that's what you want. So you're saying you don't have a problem with me flirting with other girls." He watches me, his body still, his expression unreadable.

"You're a free agent."

He sighs and shakes his head. "Tell me, what part of boyfriend and girlfriend don't you understand?"

"All of it." I jump up and walk away, rubbing my arms.

He stands. "Perhaps I'd better be going. It seems you can only take the couple thing in small bites." He smiles but his voice is strained.

Hesitantly, I reach up and touch his cheek. Besides my family, this is the closest I've ever let anyone get. "I do like you, Tyler." And then some, if the way my heart speeds up every time he's around is anything to go by.

He takes my hand, kisses the palm, and closes my fingers around it. "I know you do. I just wasn't sure you'd figured it out. I'll see you tomorrow." He turns and with long, loose-limbed strides disappears around the side of the house.

As soon as I hear his car motor, I hurry in to get my knife before I go into the ocean. Better to be safe than sorry. I fasten the scabbard to my leg and trot out. The sound of dishes clicking and water splashing drifts from the kitchen. "I'm going to the ocean, Gramps."

"Tyler gone?" he calls back.

I head to the kitchen and stand in the doorway. "Yeah."

"How's that going?"

"It's complicated."

"Relationships always are."

There is that R word again. "Yeah."

He glances up and sees my swimsuit and the knife. "Are you going back to where you saw the research vessel?" His expression is troubled.

While I've managed to keep thoughts of the research vessel at bay all day, the fear it brings with it comes back full force, crawling like sludge through my system. "I have to. They might have caught another dolphin."

"Better a dolphin than you." He turns back to his dishes. Gramps might not like it, but he won't waste his breath trying to talk me out of it. Gramps has one rule he lives by. Do what's right. We both know freeing a sea creature planned for experimentation is right.

I walk over, hug his waist, and lean my cheek against his back. "I'll be careful."

"See that you are." His voice gruff, he scrubs vigorously at the meatloaf pan.

I slip out the door, head for the cliff, and dive off.

As I soar through the air, my world rights and the tension tightening my shoulder blades fades. The water barely ripples when I hit it.

Dog paddling, I look around. Except for the occasional splash in the distance, it's quiet. The moon glints on the water, creating a misty sheen. I look out to sea. My breath lodges in my throat. Is that speck in the distance the vessel I saw last night?

I kick out and swim in that direction. An hour later, I'm close enough to see the ship. Blinking liquid out of my eyes, I sink into the water till only the top of my head and eyes are visible. Nothing on board moves. I let myself drop underwater and look around. My hair tickles my shoulders as it floats around me.

My heart tightens. The trap is next to the ship and holds an adult dolphin that chatters in distress.

I bite my lips and force my pounding heart to slow. Pulling out my knife, I quickly spring the lock. The dolphin chatters louder and nudges me hard with his nose, pushing me back a couple of feet as he swims free.

He shoves me again. Something's wrong. Now that he's free, he shouldn't be this agitated. My muscles tighten. My breathing shallow, I glance up. A diver!

Cursing myself for letting him take me by surprise, I shove away, fast, but he's already on me. He reaches for my foot and grabs my ankle.

A dark shadow cuts through the water nearby on my right. The feel of wet rubber hits my leg. The diver lets go as the dolphin dives between us.

With a burst of speed, I shoot through the water, intent on putting as much distance as possible between myself and the diver. I glance over my shoulder; the diver comes doggedly on, but the distance between us grows.

In the water, my reflexes, my muscles, and agility are on par with the creatures of the sea. The diver falls further and further behind.

I swim hard. By the time I feel it's safe to slow down, my heart is pounding. I glance to my right and freeze. I've attracted the attention of something more dangerous than a diver.

Chapter 17

A great white is only a few feet away. Its flat, black eyes make my heart rate accelerate and panic flood my system. Sharks scare the holy crap out of me, especially great whites. I swim slowly backward never taking my gaze off the huge shark. I read somewhere they have over three thousand teeth. Why does any fish need that many teeth?

The shark keeps pace with me. I have a strong desire to wring my hands. Where are my dolphin buddies when I need them? Not fair. I've already been saved once tonight. Plus, I don't want them to become shark fodder.

Stay calm. I force my heart rate to level. I don't want to use up my remaining oxygen too quickly. It's been a while since I've surfaced. I certainly can't now. Half an hour is my max. But if it comes to drowning or being eaten by a shark, I choose drowning.

The shark circles me. I turn with it. My head feels light from lack of oxygen. Keeping my eyes on the shark, I kick upward. I want to get as close to the surface as I can.

It swims closer. Looking deep into those soulless eyes, I know it's getting ready to attack. Panic disappears. Calm takes its place. I fist my hands, ready to fight.

It moves with unbelievable speed and beauty. Jaws wide, it comes at me.

I pull to the side and aim for its eye. My fist makes contact with its head and glances off.

I don't do any damage but it takes the shark by surprise. Those huge jaws close. He shakes his head and thrashes his tail. Always go for the eyes, gills, or nose, Gramps has said over and over. I lunge for his snout. Bringing my fists together, I hit as hard as I can.

He turns so fast, his tail knocks against my side and stomach. Reflexively, my mouth opens in a gasp. I swallow water. Burbling, I head for the surface. The shark is no longer my primary concern; I feel like I'm drowning. I shoot to the surface and gasp for air, coughing. I manage to chuff, water spilling out of my blowhole.

It's only when I can breathe again that I take a cautious look around. The shark is gone.

I've had all the adventure I can handle for one night and head home. My arms feel leaden; each breath hurts my lungs. I hope I don't encounter any more creatures in trouble, because I'm not sure I can do anything about it.

The feel of wet rubber grazes my side. I look around, alarmed, afraid the great white has come back for a snack. Relief floods me. It's my friends. Swimming on each side of me is a dolphin. I grab their fins and hold on. I'm not sure if they ran off the shark or he decided I wasn't worth the effort. Either way, I'm glad he's gone.

The dolphins carry me several miles. When I see the shore, I let go. "Thanks."

They chirp in reply. My gaze follows them as they swim back toward the middle of the ocean. Half-swimming, half-floating I make my way to the shallows, drag myself up the trail and into the house.

Gramps looks up from the murder-mystery he's reading. His feet are up and a large, empty bowl sits at his side. The smell of buttered popcorn hangs in the room. My mouth waters but the need for rest is stronger than the need for food.

"You okay?" He places a finger between the pages and closes the book.

"Just tired. I'm going to bed. I'll talk with you tomorrow." I trudge toward my bedroom. It seems a million miles away.

"Sweet dreams, Pip."

"Thanks, Gramps." Ten more steps to go, one foot after the other. I slip out of my wet suit and drop onto the bed. Sleep comes instantly.

The screeching alarm clock interrupts dreams of running from divers before morphing into a dolphin in front of Tyler.

I stumble into the tiny bathroom off my bedroom. "Crap." In the middle of my ablutions it dawns on me I haven't done my homework. "Oh well." I'll have to beg forgiveness and turn it in late, an automatic grade drop. I dress, and hurry to the kitchen, my stomach rumbling like a freight train. My mouth waters at the scent of oatmeal and coffee.

"Thanks, Gramps." I drop into my seat and take a swig of coffee. My world rights the moment I swallow the hot caffeine. I turn my attention to my oatmeal.

Gramps lets me get halfway through before he queries, "Anything happen last night?" He folds the morning paper and sets it aside.

"You don't miss much do you?" I smile and devour another couple of bites.

His movements stiff, he picks up my bowl, fills it up, and sets it in front of me.

"Thanks, Gramps." I sip my coffee. "I went back to the boat. They'd caught another dolphin. This time when I freed it a diver came after me." I don't mention the shark. No point putting my only relative on sensory overload.

He sits down, folds his hands. "And?" His voice and mannerism are calm but he can't hide the worry in his eyes.

"The dolphin acted as a buffer and I got away. The diver followed me but he couldn't keep up," I mumble around a mouthful of oatmeal. I'm finally losing that hollow feeling in the pit of my stomach. I glance at the clock. "Got to run, or I'll be late for school. Don't worry, okay?" I shove back from the table, kiss the top of his head, and bolt.

Beulah and I roar down the hill in a cloud of white exhaust. I pull into the parking lot and slow when I see an open spot next to Fahrenbacher's muscle car, shrug and drive to the next row where there are several parking spaces. I have enough irons in the fire—such as dolphins—to worry about, without adding a pissed-off Fahrenbacher into the mix.

After getting out of the truck, I trot into school. Tyler's waiting inside the foyer. He disentangles himself from his entourage and steps forward, a wide smile on his face. He reaches for my hand. I yank it back. "What are you doing?"

He rolls his eyes. "That's what people do who go together."

My head swivels in his direction. I can only hope the tinted glasses hide my anxiety. From the look on his face, maybe not. In between saving dolphins and being attacked by divers and sharks, this couple thing is a lot to deal with. Not that I intend to mention any of the many complications in my life to my new boyfriend.

"Not us. No one is supposed to know, remember?" Hadn't he agreed to that? I frown, trying to remember. You'd think I'm Gramps' age and having a senior moment instead of a teenager. Actually, Gramps' memory is twice as good as mine.

"I was hoping we'd gotten past that." He falls into step beside me as I hurry down the hall, waiting for the sound of the bell.

"Gotten past it? We only became an item last night." I look around to make sure no one hears.

"Ashamed of me, huh?" he teases.

Ashamed of him? If he only knew. I'd love to hang a banner in the gym that says in big bold letters Tyler Carlisle is Piper's guy. But given the fact he doesn't know I'm a mutant, that's really not an option. "Will you stop?" I rush into the classroom and head for my spot in the back of the classroom, beside his sister.

Sitting with Holly is almost as bad. She's nearly as popular as her brother. But no one thinks too much about our association, probably because Holly is nice to everyone.

I slide into my seat and plop my book bag onto the chair's left-handed arm. Tyler sinks into the seat beside me.

"Go away," I whisper.

He makes a point to look around. "No seats available."

"What about that one on the front row?"

"Looks like Ted Johnson just snagged it." He gives me an unrepentant look.

Holly watches us curiously.

Miss Sweeney walks in, putting an end to the bickering.

I stare straight ahead and try to concentrate, but it's an effort in futility. Tyler's legs are spread in that classic way males have of taking up their leg space and that of the person next to them. Our knees touch. I inch away, doing my best to ignore how such casual contact overloads my circuits and sends a sharp charge of electricity along my nerve endings.

Out of the corner of my eye, I glance at Tyler. If he's aware of his impact on me he certainly doesn't show it.

It doesn't help that Holly keeps eyeing us with a smug expression on her pretty face. Has he told her or hasn't he?

The only positive in the entire fifty minutes is Miss Sweeney doesn't call on me. One has to appreciate blessings no matter how small.

The minute the bell rings, I jump up and make a dash for the hall. Or try to. Holly stands in my way. I nudge her aside with a well-placed elbow.

Tyler looks like he has every intention of following me until one of his admirers steps in and clutches his arm. Should I be jealous? I'm too relieved to worry about it. I bolt with Holly at my heels.

"So," Holly begins.

"Don't say a word."

"But…"

"Not a word."

She grumbles beside me, arms clasp around her books, as we scurry to our next class. For the rest of the day I only see Tyler at a distance, always surrounded by a bevy of pretty giggling girls. Once when he catches me looking, he winks at me before turning his attention to the redhead at his elbow.

Holly hears me mutter under my breath. "I'm not saying a word," she responds.

I roll my eyes and bump into my nemesis.

"Carlisle's not going to be around all the time," he warns and knocks against my shoulder hard enough to make me wince.

I feel heat behind my eyes and get in his face. "Bring it on, Fahrenbacher. Any time, any place."

He throws back his head and blinks. He stares at me and I stare back. A slow grin spreads across his face and for the first time I understand his appeal—in an abstract way. "Maybe you're not such a mouse after all. I like a female with spirit." He chucks me under the chin. Before I can bat his hand away, he drops it and saunters off.

Open-mouthed, I stare after him, shaking my head, and wondering if the whole world has run mad.

Eyes wide, Holly watches him walk away. A broad smile splits her face. "You go, girl."

Chapter 18

The rest of the day passes uneventfully. I hate to admit it, but I'm upset Tyler hasn't made more of an effort to seek me out. When the bell rings, I hurry to my truck. Tyler is leaning against the fender, ear buds in, listening to his iPod.

A smile of pleasure ripples across my face before I manage to get it under control. As if sensing my presence, Tyler looks up and smiles back, removing the ear buds.

"Hey." He pushes off Beulah.

"Hey yourself."

"Let's go get a latte." His hands run down my arms and cup my fingers.

For a moment, I'm oblivious to the other kids pouring into the parking lot, throwing curious looks our way.

A dark-haired sophomore with acne jostles my elbow. "Excuse me." No doubt she'd been too busy staring at Tyler to pay attention to where she was going. But it's enough to bring me back to my surroundings. I withdraw my hands.

"I'm not sure it's such a good idea." I begin moving back out of arms reach.

"You're going to turn down a latte?" He raises his eyebrows in exaggerated disbelief. "Come on, I deserve to be rewarded. I followed your instructions to the letter. I haven't seen you since first hour." He leans forward and draws me toward him.

"Yeah, I can tell that's a hardship." Regretfully, I shrug off his hands.

"Hmm, if I lifted those glasses, would I find your eyes green?" he teases.

I lean away from him.

"Come on, Piper," he urges. "Holly will be there, along with half the school. No one will think anything about it. And why should you care if they do?"

There it is again. That thinly-veiled demand for knowledge of my secret. Why can't he let it be?

His glance goes from good-humored to edgy. Suddenly, I decide to give him this round and hope he'll forget about my secrets.

"Let's go."

He looks startled. In that instant, I realize he hadn't thought I'd go. "If you don't want to…"

His eyes light and he gives me that crooked grin.

My heart ka-thumps.

He grabs my hand and we walk down the block. Since most of the crowd has cleared out, I don't pull away immediately. It feels too right. I am such a goner.

"Piper,"

"Hmm?" I watch a stray cat skitter across the street out of harm's way as a car goes barreling by.

"How were you able to save me during the storm?"

"What do you mean?" My muscles tighten and my gait becomes stiff. I've been dreading this question. When he didn't ask in the beginning, I thought I was going to luck out. I should have known better.

"Why didn't you drown out there?"

I glance at him from behind my glasses before looking quickly away. "Why didn't you?"

"If you hadn't rescued me, I'm sure I would have. How did you do it?"

"I'm a strong swimmer." I trip on a crack in the sidewalk and blush with embarrassment. Outside of the water, grace is not my middle name.

"You're on Olympian level then."

I shrug.

"I want to understand," he presses.

"What do you want me to say, I've got super powers?" I snap, pulling my hand away.

"Do you?"

I giggle in spite of myself. I like to pretend I'm a superhero, but there's a big difference between mutant DNA and superpowers.

Tyler smiles reluctantly.

"Can't you just say thank you and let it go?"

Tyler sighs. "Thank you. I saw Fahrenbacher talking to you."

I appreciate the change of subject. I know this isn't easy for him. Heck, we're teenagers. While it may not be listed on the teenage manifesto, anyone in our age bracket is curious to the point of being downright nosy. It appears Tyler is no exception. Though I'm afraid it goes deeper than that. He's mixing up emotion with curiosity, trying to bring it down to a trust level. For both our sakes, I hope he never gives me an ultimatum.

"Yeah, I told him I'd clean his clock if he bothered me again. He decided he likes a female with spirit." I snort.

Tyler grins and shakes his head. "He better not decide he likes you too much or I'll be the one doing the clock cleaning."

"Again. You aren't the jealous type are you?"

We've arrived at the Pink Cat. Before I can reach for the door, Tyler opens it. "I'm mild-mannered but I am the jealous type."

I frown as I walk through the door, puzzling that one out. "You won't go all caveman on me will you?"

"No promises, but I'll do my best."

"I can see this relationship thing is going to be complicated." I sigh.

The noise level rises several decibels when we cross the threshold. He leans down close to my ear so I can hear him. "I'll make it as easy on you as I can."

His breath sends a flutter through me. I'm so susceptible to this boy. Just think of him like a virus, I tell myself. Eventually, I'll be immune and able to deal with him with equanimity.

"Piper. Tyler. Over here." Holly waves her arm from a nearby booth. We've taken two steps in that direction when Tyler gets waylaid by a couple of girls in his science class. I keep going. I reach the booth and scoot Holly over with my hip.

"The bench on the other side is empty," she points out before taking a long sip of what looks to be a caramel frappuccino.

"Stating the obvious," I mumble.

"What's going on between you and my brother?" Holly waves at some girls from first hour two tables over.

"What do you mean," I respond cautiously.

"Come on, Piper. Ever since you rescued him—"

"I didn't rescue him."

"Whatever." She shrugs. "Ever since the rescue, things have been different. And don't think I'm the only one who's noticed."

Crap. I'm strongly tempted to put my head on the table and howl. What am I doing here anyway? This is hardly inconspicuous. Led astray by the lure of lattes. I sigh. And speaking of which, I start to rise. "I've got to get my latte."

"I don't think that will be necessary." Holly points. Weaving his way through the crowd, Tyler has nearly reached our table, two lattes in hand.

My world brightens. I sink back down.

Tyler sets a drink in front of me and slides into the opposite booth. He looks at me sitting next to his sister. His left eyebrow shoots up. I ignore him, my attention focused on the latte.

I reach for it and take a long sip. Espresso and mocha tease my senses in an icy wavy of pleasure. I close my eyes and let my muscles go lax. "Thank you."

When I open them, Tyler is staring at me with a bemused expression. "What?"

"Your voice."

The cold milk has coated my esophagus and even though I lowered it, the words came out smoother than usual. "What about it?" I add in my normal husky tones.

"It sounds like it's wrapped in silk."

"Eww, Tyler, my ears. Is that one of your normal pickup lines?" Holly wrinkles her nose.

Bless Holly. I relax. And ask, curious, "Does my voice have any effect on you?"

"Pa-lease."

Interesting. It must be a male thing.

Tyler leans forward. "You seriously don't notice the sensual cadence of each word that ripples from her lips?"

"Stop." She claps her hands over her ears. "Piper is a friend of mine."

"Maybe it's your imagination."

"Imagination or not, your voice has an effect on me that I don't dare talk about in front of my sister."

"You keep this up and I'm going to go sit with friends," she threatens.

"Don't let us stop you." He leans back and stretches his legs, his knees touching mine.

"Stay put, Holly," I order, shifting my legs.

"Are you two an item?" Her glance shifts back and forth between the two of us.

"No."

"Yes," he says at the same time.

He gives me a pained look.

"Yes, but no one is supposed to know about it." I make circles with my drink on the table, not meeting anyone's eye.

"Why?"

"I'm trying to keep a low profile. To be perfectly honest spending time with you doesn't help."

"Why are you trying to keep a low profile?" She tilts her head, her expression puzzled.

"Good luck getting that one answered." Tyler picks up his drink and finishes it with one long sip.

"I have my reasons," I mutter and shift in my seat.

"I'm sure they're good ones. Tyler, leave her alone. If it's something she wants you to know she'll tell you."

A lump rises in my throat. I blink my eyes to keep the moisture back. Is this what it's like to have a friend? Someone to show unwavering support whether they understand or not? "Thanks, Holly."

"What are friends for? I appreciate you spending time with me even though it gets in the way of your low profile." She gives me a quick hug before whispering to Tyler, "What do you think, homeland security or witness protection?"

In unison, they turn and study me, their expressions so alike it's scary. It must be a twin thing. I hold up my hand. "Don't even go there."

But of course, once she's opened that can of worms the next forty minutes is spent on endless speculation of my low profile, each suggestion more outrageous than the one before. Though mutant is never mentioned. Thank goodness.

I listen to their nonsense another ten minutes before scooting out of the booth.

Holly and Tyler stand, too. I motion them down. "Stay put, I've got to go." Before long, the sun will be down. I need to check on the dolphins. I have no intention of letting the research vessel capture one of my friends.

"I need to get home. I've got four chapters of history to read." Holly takes one last noisy sip of her drink.

"I'll see you tomorrow." I nod at Tyler.

"I'll walk you back to your truck." Tyler unfolds his lanky frame and stands up.

"That's not necessary," I protest, torn between feeling warm all the way down to my toes because I'll be spending a few more minutes with him and wondering how to keep some distance between us.

He looks at me and waits patiently.

I shrug. "Fine."

He reaches for my hand. I notice two girls in my social science class watching us and hastily pull it away.

He scowls and lets his drop to his side. As we walk toward the door, one of the girls gets up and plants herself in front of him. "Hi, Tyler."

I keep walking.

"Piper," he calls after me.

I pretend not to hear. I hurry out the door and walk with my head down. This is so awkward. He's so damn hot. I could resist the hotness if there weren't so many other qualities about Tyler I like. He's confident and comfortable with himself. He tries to do right by other people. I'd say he's nice, but nice is such a bland term. It's more than that. He genuinely cares about people.

I'm in such a brown study, I'm not even aware he's caught up with me till he slips his hand around mine. I try to jerk it back, but he doesn't let go.

"Someone may see us," I say, but as usual, his slightest touch weakens my resolve.

"And that would be a problem because? Oh yes, witness protection."

I roll my eyes and he grins, his eyes twinkling with mischief. As he swings my hand, I sigh in defeat. "You aren't making this easy you know," I complain.

"Give me a reason to and I'll be the soul of rectitude."

I stop and look at him. "How about because I ask you to?"

He drops my hand. "You don't play fair." His voice is strained.

I touch his arm lightly. "I'm sorry if this is difficult for you. This is a really big step for me. I'm with you because…"

"You can't help yourself," he says almost bitterly. "Your body wants me whether you do or not."

"You are so full of yourself," I say angrily and stomp away, knowing he's right. He's not full of himself and my body does want him. Damn teenage hormones.

He catches up with me in two long easy strides. "Don't mind me. I'm just in a bad mood because you left me with Barbie the Man Eater back there."

I giggle. He grins back. "The only thing I've got to grumble about is I'm going with the hottest babe in school and absolutely no one knows about it."

We reach my truck before I realize it. I grab for the door, but in one quick movement, he's pinned me. I take a quick look around but the lot is empty.

"But there is an upside to that." He traps my body against the truck, his arms on either side of my head, his lips close to mine.

The fear of being seen fades. We aren't visible from this side of the truck, I rationalize. As his body presses against mine, I go limp. "What's that?"

He pulls off my glasses. His warm breath fans my face. I breathe in chocolate and coffee.

"I've got a clear playing field without having to fight off a few hundred males with raging testosterone."

"Well that's good, since one's all I can handle," I manage to get out before his lips close over mine. His warm mouth moves persuasively, his tongue slides between my teeth and does a dance with mine. His hard body presses against me.

I slide my arms around his waist, tightening my grip, pressing back. The kiss escalates, his hands move from the truck to slide down my body, scalding me wherever they touch.

Slowly, reluctantly, he pulls away, gasping.

My breasts heave. Everything's spinning.

With a lopsided grin, he hands me my glasses. I start to put them on upside down and catch them before they fall off my face. He laughs, takes them from me, and places them carefully on my face.

"Like I said, the hottest girl in school."

I look down at my shapeless clothes and shake my head.

He grins. "I know what's under them. Actually, I find it rather titillating." His cell phone rings. He pulls it out, still watching me. "Yeah, Mom. On my way."

"Supper's ready. Mom's calling to remind me she's fixed my favorite."

"And that would be?" My breath is now under control.

"Spaghetti. Better go." He kisses me on the nose and walks to his car.

I get in my truck and slam the door. There's just no quiet way to close Beulah's doors. Tyler starts his car. I follow him out.

As I pull out of the lot, I glance across the street. That's when I see Fahrenbacher's car.

Chapter 19

"Damn it." I hit the steering wheel with the side of my fist. Acid spurts in my stomach. Of all the people I didn't want to see that kiss, Fahrenbacher heads the list. "Maybe he didn't see us," I console myself. But my luck doesn't run that way. Of course he saw us. I continue to mutter the rest of the way home then paste on a smile so Gramps won't know I'm upset.

I need not have bothered. Gramps has bigger fish to fry.

"Are you going out again tonight to see if the dolphin hunters are out there?" is his opening gambit over dinner.

"I've got to check it out. They could have captured one of my relatives," I mumble around a huge bite of mac and cheese.

"I don't like it. Thinking of you ending up in one of those labs turns my hair gray."

"Your hair is already gray," I point out helpfully, swallowing the rest of my cheesy macaroni.

"Smart mouth," he grumbles. "I might as well try to stop the wind from blowing as to try to talk you out of something you've got your mind set on. Your mom was the same way." I notice the stains under his eyes and the sallowness of his skin.

"Are you feeling okay?"

"Don't try to change the subject, missy."

I reach over and clasp his hand, rough and warm in mine. "The last thing in the world I want to do is cause you worry. If you want me to stay at home, I will." I have to force the words out. It will kill me if something happens to the dolphins that I could prevent.

Gramps gives me a long look then sighs. His shoulders slump. He knows it. "I can't ask you to be less than you are." He straightens and gives a determined grin.

"But I can do my best to keep you safe." He pushes away from the table, walks out of the kitchen, and comes back a moment later carrying a small bag. He thrusts it at me.

"What's this?"

"Open it and find out."

The bag rustles as I pick it up.

"Open it," he urges again. His hands in his back pockets, he rocks back and forth on his heels.

I smile and peep inside. Two blue boxes that look like watch boxes are nestled in the bottom of the sack. I pick one up and turn the box around in my hand. "Did you get us matching watches?" I'm only half-joking.

He just smiles, waiting for me to open the box.

I pop the top, bemused. It's a large watch with a picture screen and lots of buttons. I raise my eyebrows.

Impatient, he sits down, pulls out the other box, and opens it. It's an identical watch. "It's a GPS system."

"Oh. That's nice." I smile my appreciation, still at sea as to why he'd get us matching GPS watches. Good thing I don't worry about making fashion statements. This certainly won't do it.

"It works in the water."

"Oh." The light goes on.

He starts pushing buttons and leans over to show me. "It has a panic button. Press the first button on the right."

I do as instructed. A red light pulses on his watch. "Press the button if you're in trouble. It gives me your coordinates. Same goes with mine. If I get in trouble, yours starts blinking."

"I'm thrilled to have this, but don't even talk about getting in trouble. I couldn't bear it if something happened to you."

"Don't worry, honey, I intend to live a good long time." He pats my shoulder. "But enough of that. If for any reason you think you're running into trouble, press the button. I'll come out in the boat and get you."

Touched, I reach over and kiss his rough cheek. A wisp of soft whiskers tickles my mouth. "Thanks, Gramps. This is the best gift I've ever had."

"You're welcome. Now if you still think you need to go, you better get going before it gets any later."

Since the sun is setting and I don't want Gramps to worry, I should go. I push back my chair and hurry to my bedroom to change. A few minutes later I'm in a downward dive off the cliff.

The warm wind whips around me, blowing my hair to the side. My hands cut the water and my body follows them down. The water caresses me, circling me like embryonic fluid. I grasp my knees, roll in a ball, and turn over and over, smiling with joy. I give myself five minutes to play before I strike out in the direction I've seen the boat in the past. I check my new watch. It's taken me fifty minutes to reach the general area. The water darkens as the sun sets.

Before I even reach the boat, I sense the distressed chattering of at least two dolphins. Like the dolphins, I use echolocation under water. I pick up the high-pitched vibration, which is generated in their forehead, along my jawbone. My jawbone conducts sound like my ears do, at least when I'm underwater. By the frequencies I'm getting, it sounds like two dolphins, a male and a female about a mile up ahead. I extend my arms and swim faster.

In a few minutes, I spot the shadowy outline of the cage. The slightly larger male dolphin is caught inside, while the female swims in agitated circles around the cage, chattering.

I look around. When I see nothing but shadows, I pull out the knife strapped to my ankle and pry open the door. In a flash, the dolphin darts through. Both dolphins glide a distance away and continue their chatter. Something's wrong. I sense it.

As the dolphins' agitation mounts, I turn in a slow circle. That's when I see the three divers.

Chapter 20

I've seriously ticked someone off. I punch the panic button on my watch and take off, using long fast strokes that pull me quickly through the water. Unfortunately, the divers are no slouches. I do a quick glance over my shoulder. The man in the middle motions the others to fan out.

This isn't good. Even if I outswim them, and I should be able to, there are now three swimmers that have seen me swimming underwater without scuba equipment. And they, along with Rick Sabatini, know what I look like. Thank goodness for my nerd disguise.

Where do I go? I can't lead them to my home. Instead of heading inland, I switch directions, not going out to sea but swimming horizontal to the coast, still several miles out.

I glance upward. If I can hold on till Gramps gets here with the boat, hopefully, I can make my escape. Kicking hard, I pull ahead, but not far enough. I continue to swim and they continue to trail behind me in a V, almost as if herding me.

My lungs are screaming for oxygen. I need to break the surface and chuff, but they're close enough they might see what I'm doing. Plus, it would give them time to catch up. I can't let them see the blowhole. If they do, they'll track me mercilessly and I'll end up dead or a lab rat.

I'm starting to flag. It's harder and harder to breathe. They're closing in. I'm beginning to feel disoriented. The water is cold. Even swimming, I'm shivering.

Suddenly, another diver appears in front of me. His tawny hair ripples up from his head, creating a halo effect. It must be the lack of oxygen. He points to the surface. I'm confused. He swims closer. Tyler!

Another diver drops down near me. Gramps! He too motions to the surface. I push upward and break the surface. My lungs on fire, I gasp for air. I pull myself onto the ladder of Gramps' boat and chuff. Now that I'm not in immediate danger of drowning I need to go back and check on

Gramps and Tyler. They might need my help. I'm lowering myself off the ladder as their heads surface. Relief washes over me.

"Get on the boat, girl." The urgency in Gramps voice propels me up the side and over. Gramps follows with Tyler at his heels. "Take the wheel, while I get out of this rubber suit will you?" He stands, dripping, a few feet away. I hurry to obey.

Tyler follows me, his fins slapping the wooden deck. "Are you all right?" He grabs me to him and hugs me, his wet suit cold and clammy.

"Yes. I need to steer the boat." My voice is muffled against his chest.

He drops his arms and I hurry toward the wheel and throttle up. The boat's motor breaks the quiet of the night. Stars shine down, lighting a path. I leave the running lights off in case anyone is following us. My hands on the wheel, I ask, "What happened down there? Are they following us? Did they try to hurt you?" Nerves make my teeth chatter, I tighten my grip on the wheel.

"They apparently weren't expecting anyone but a lone girl. When they saw us, they took off."

I wonder what the divers would have done if they'd realized they'd been up against a dolph-girl, a boy, and an old man. Thank goodness we didn't have to find out.

"What are you doing here, Tyler?"

"More to the point, what are you?" He drops to the bench and pulls off a flipper, then the other.

"I asked first."

"Let me get out of this suit, and then we'll talk." He disappears down the steps but is back moments later. I take a quick glance in his direction. He's wearing khaki shorts and a plain white T-shirt. I'd like to scoop him up with a spoon, he looks so yummy.

"I came to visit you. About the time I got to the door, your grandpa came rushing out saying he got a distress call from you. By the way, how did you give him a distress call in the middle of the ocean?" he interrupts himself.

I point proudly to my new watch.

He comes over and checks it out. Like any male, he's distracted by a new gadget. "I gotta get one of these." He moves my wrist this way and that.

Gramps comes up behind us. In the light of the moon, his face looks gray.

"Are you okay, Gramps?"

"Fine, why wouldn't I be?"

Why indeed? Another male trait, they never want to appear less than firm, fit, and macho.

"The watch worked like a charm."

"It did, didn't it?" He grins wide, his teeth white in the dark.

"Is it safe to head home?"

"Yeah, I think so. Go straight to the town dock. We'll blend."

I look at the boat's GPS and turn the wheel a bit to the right. "You made good time."

Tyler chimes in. "He drove like a maniac. No disrespect, Mr. Dunn."

Gramps chuckles.

"Does someone want to tell me what's going on?" Tyler looks from me to Gramps and back.

Gramps nudges me away and takes the wheel. "Why don't you two talk. I'll navigate."

"Thanks, Gramps." I shoot him a look. He winks at me.

Tyler holds out his hand. I clasp it and we walk to the stern. The night is beautiful. The moon is out, its light reflected on the small lapping waves of the ocean. The stars shine like twinkling diamonds in the heavens. Very romantic. But at the moment, I'm afraid romance is the last thing on Tyler's mind. He wants answers. Answers I'm not prepared to give.

Chapter 21

Our arms on the rail, we stare at the dark, rippling water. Tyler holds a clenched fist to his mouth and coughs. "Are you going to tell me what happened?"

"I found a dolphin that had been trapped, harvested. I freed it."

"I get that. What I don't get is how you can swim under water without gear."

"It takes practice." I shrug.

He snorts. "Yeah, right. Piper, relationships require trust. I trusted you enough to tell you about my Mafia uncle."

Easy for him to say. He may have Mafia family members but he doesn't run the risk of being put in a lab, strapped to a table, and cut on.

"I'm here for you when you need me and I always will be. I'm falling hard for you, Piper." He turns and angles toward me, his expression intense. Even though we aren't touching, I feel his heat.

"I agreed to be your girl. Isn't that enough?" I look straight out to sea when I speak.

"Agreed to?" he asks, an edge to his voice.

"You know what I mean." I feel caught between desperation and exasperation. I'm so not good at this. How do I tell him he warms my heart and makes my toes curl? The words stick in my throat. Communicating my feelings is so not my strong suit.

"No, I don't."

Instead of mentioning curling toes and warm heart, all I say is, "I care about you. You are the only one I'd risk a relationship with. Isn't that enough?"

He gives me a strained smile. "Trust me, being mysterious isn't all it's cracked up to be."

I look at him, incredulous. "Is that what you think this is, me adding a little mystery? Trying to spice things up?"

He gives me a crooked grin. "Spicing things up certainly isn't an issue."

I smile, relieved. Maybe things will be all right.

We motor into the harbor. Gramps shuts down the engine and we head for the truck. I sit in the middle. Tyler stares out the window, making no effort to talk.

"We can take care of the dolphins, honey." Gramps pats my knee.

I clear my dry throat. I'm not sure why I feel close to tears. "How's that?"

"We get word to the fishing community some big conglomerate is trying to harvest them. It's bad for the tourist industry. And a lot of the fisherman won't like it on a personal level."

I straighten and clap my hands. "Gramps, that's brilliant."

He grumbles. "I'm getting old, I should have thought of it before now."

"So, this isn't the first time this has happened." Tyler breaks his silence.

"Third," Gramps responds.

"You've been out there three nights in a row?" Tyler's eyebrows shoot up.

"Well, it won't be necessary for her to go out again," Gramps responds bracingly.

Tyler subsides back into brooding silence.

As soon as the truck pulls in, Tyler opens the door and walks to his car.

"Tyler," I call.

He looks back. "Yes?"

"I'll see you tomorrow." I drop the hand I've raised.

"Sure." He gets in, flashes his lights, and heads down the drive.

"Is there a problem with love's young dream?" Gramps ask as he ambles toward the door.

Eww. "What a disgusting expression." I slip my hands in the pockets of my cargo pants.

"He usually takes every opportunity to steal a kiss instead of driving off in a huff."

"Oh, Gramps." Heat floods my face. It's probably red enough to glow like a neon sign.

"It's none of my business." He unlocks the front door before reaching in and turning on the lights.

"I suck at relationships," I complain. My bare feet slap across the floor.

"You've never been in one before." He points out the obvious.

"He got in a snit because I wouldn't tell him what I am. He thinks I'm trying to be mysterious."

"Young men get their egos damaged pretty easily. They're a delicate thing, young male egos. And as far as what you are, you're a beautiful girl. Or I guess I should say woman. Though, I prefer to think of you as a girl." As we walk through the kitchen, he grabs a chair and leans against it.

"Are you all right?" My muscles knot. I stare at him anxiously. "Please say you're all right."

"Of course I am." He straightens and gives me a reassuring smile. "Things just aren't usually this exciting around here. Now you better get your homework done and get to bed."

"You go to bed, too." I don't like his color. "Why don't you make an appointment with Doc Johnson?"

"That old quack," he scoffs. "He'd like nothing better than to poke and prod me. Probably draw more blood than a vampire."

"Please." I hold his arm.

He sighs and caves. "If it will make you feel better. I'll make an appointment tomorrow."

"Don't forget."

"You won't let me. Goodnight now."

"Goodnight, Gramps." I give him one more searching look, kiss his cheek, and head to my room.

Screw homework. Fatigue drags at me. I tumble into bed and fall immediately asleep.

Birds chirping wake me the next morning. A good thing, too, I've got a quiz in Soc. I hop out of bed, throw on clothes, and crack open my book. I skim the information. I'm good to go.

Gramps is sitting at the table, his hands wrapped around a cup of coffee. "Hi, honey." He looks exhausted.

"Hi, Gramps." I walk over and kiss his stubbly cheek.

"I've been lazy this morning. Think you can make do with cold cereals?"

Warning bells go off. Gramps is never lazy. "Not a problem, I just want coffee anyway. I need to get to school early to study."

"You should eat something."

"I think I'll treat myself to an Egg McMuffin."

He nods. "That works."

"You're going to call the doctor, aren't you?"

"Yeah." He sips his coffee and sets it down.

"Promise?"

"Promise."

"Call me if you need anything."

"Of course."

"Have a good day." I take a gulp of the steaming beverage and head toward the door. I stop in the doorway and look back. He gives me a reassuring smile.

I wave my fingers at him and head out the door.

It's only after I'm at school I realize I forgot my GPS watch. I know Gramps got it for me but he said he could use it, too.

"He has his phone," I assure myself.

"Talking to yourself now, Dunn?" Fahrenbacher slows his step to mine as I hurry down the hall.

"What's it to you?" I snap. I'm not in the mood to take any crap from Edgar the Asshole today.

"Feisty. My kind of woman." He steps closer, invading my space.

"Don't you have some flies you need to pull wings off of?" I retort and pick up my pace.

"Hmm, while that sounds entertaining, I'd rather spend my time with you."

"Rather torment me is what you're saying."

"Actually, that's no longer as appealing as other things I could do with you."

I stop and stare at him. "Are you insane?"

"I saw Tyler plant a hot and heavy one on you last night. From where I was at it looked like he used plenty of tongue. There must be something hidden beneath that mousy exterior and I plan on finding out what it is." He smirks.

Damn it. Damn it. Damn it. "I don't know what you're talking about." I continue determinedly forward. He paces at my side.

"Of course, you don't." He smiles knowingly.

"I liked you better when you were just rude and mean. And I didn't like you at all then."

"A challenge. I enjoy a challenge."

I shake my head. This is too bizarre. There's no way my stars are aligned.

Chapter 22

"Hey, Piper." Holly hurries up behind me. I blink. Rick Sabatini is loping at her side. I want to bang my head against the wall and howl. A quick glance assures me his attention is all for Holly.

"Edgar." She slides smoothly between us. I have to move to the side since Sabatini is adhered to her like glue.

"How are you, Holly?" he responds.

Several disgusted looks are thrown in our direction. We're taking up most of the hallway but no one wants to anger Fahrenbacher or get on the bad side of the new girl.

Holly turns to me. "Better pick up the pace. Class starts in four minutes."

Edgar looks directly at me. "I'll be seeing you," he says before he lopes off towards his class.

"Oh joy," I mutter to his back.

"What was that about?" Holly asks.

"He's decided on a new method of torture for me. Instead of beating me up, he wants to"—I search for the right word: Seduce? Rape? Who knows. I settle on—"get to know me better."

She raises her eyebrows. "Won't Tyler love that?"

We hurry into the classroom and sit in two available seats next to each other. Sabatini sighs and wanders to the front of the classroom where seats are always available.

I look around, spot Tyler, and smile. He gives me a cool nod.

I sigh. What now? Relationships are so complicated. I turn my attention to Miss Sweeney who today is talking about Romeo and Juliet. Not one of my favorite couples. It's not that I don't appreciate a romantic gesture as much as the next person, but to kill yourself because your significant other's dead? What's the sense in that?

I occasionally glance at Tyler, but he never makes eye contact. Something is up. When the class ends and he turns to chat with the redhead next to him, I get seriously concerned. I follow Holly out. He makes no attempt to catch up.

I'm starting to get pissed. I'm not sure what I've done to deserve this. Maybe he's taking me for a ride after all. Surely it's not because I won't tell him my secret.

Well, what's good for the goose is good for the gander. I make no further effort to see my supposed boyfriend. If this is what a relationship is, I'm not sure I want it. I fight the pain underneath the anger. My heart doesn't really hurt. That would be totally silly. I just have indigestion.

Several times, I feel him stealing glances at me. I ignore him as completely as he did me.

When the last bell rings, I head out. Tyler is standing at the door, kids streaming by him. As I start to walk by him, he falls into step beside me.

"Hey."

I ignore him.

He takes my arm and tugs me out of the way of the kids hurrying out. We stop on the edge of the sidewalk.

"Are you okay?" he asks.

"Fine." I snap.

"Are you upset?"

"No, but you obviously are. And I have no idea why."

"Don't you?"

"No. I don't."

"It's pretty evident this relationship doesn't mean as much to you as it does to me."

"That's so not true."

"Isn't it?"

We stare at each other.

"No," I respond hotly, my nails clenched into my fist.

"You're like some mystery woman. You hide the fact you're beautiful. You even change your voice. What's going on? You always hold a part of yourself back. I don't know who you are. A relationship demands trust."

I go cold inside. It's come to this. "I shouldn't have to. If you—" I can't bring myself to use the L word. It's not something Gramps and I ever say, we just know it. "If you care about me like you say you do, it wouldn't be necessary. You'd trust me and it would be enough. Apparently, my definition of caring is different from yours." I turn and walk stiffly away, my bones brittle as if they could snap on me if I move too hastily.

I feel the weight of his hot gaze but keep moving. It's over.

"Piper," he calls. I keep going. I was a fool to ever let myself get into a relationship. I'm going to fall apart and I want to be home when I do it. I want to get to Gramps.

I make it to my truck and climb into the seat. Hunched over the steering wheel, I grip it, biting my lips together. "I will not cry. I will not cry." I keep repeating the mantra, anxious to get to my grandparent. He'll offer some words of wisdom, put everything in perspective and even if I still hurt like hell, I'll feel better than I do now. And there are my dolphins to think about. Who'll protect them if I fall apart?

I jack up the volume of the radio, hoping to drown the pain. My head misses the ceiling as I turn onto the dirt lane and hit the pothole no one has bothered to fix. "Almost there, almost there." My lips mutter the words in time to the music.

Finally, I'm home. I jump out of the truck, slam the door, and run to the house. "Gramps." My voice cracks. I stop and take a deep breath. No point in letting him know how upset I am. "Gramps." My voice still sounds a little crackly. I give a little cough and try again. "Gramps."

There's no answer. I'm starting to get a little freaked. His truck is outside. Maybe he's in the back. I look outside, no Gramps. Now, I'm seriously worried. I head to the living room; there's no sign of him. My pulse rate picks up and my heart starts to beat hard. "Gramps."

I run to the kitchen. "Gramps." There's a pot of water sitting on the stove, boiling. Pasta sits next to it. I turn it off.

Maybe he's just in the bathroom. I rush to the tiny bathroom and knock on the door. "Gramps?"

No answer here either. I feel lightheaded.

I race to his bedroom and screech to a halt in the doorway. "Gramps!" I scream.

Chapter 23

He lies crumpled on the floor. The bed shadows him from the rays of sun coming through the window. Above his head, his distress watch dangles from the nightstand.

My fingers tremble so badly, I can barely dial 9-1-1. The dispatcher answers.

"Please come quick. I think my grandfather's had a heart attack. Please hurry."

"What's your name and your address?"

"This is Piper Dunn. I'm at Four Twenty-five Cliffside. Please hurry." I click off and squat down beside Gramps. "Gramps, can you hear me?"

No answer. His eyes remain closed. He's lying on his stomach, his legs and arms sprawled, his head turned to the side. I bend down and stick my finger under his nose. I feel a trickle of warm air.

Thank God. At least he's alive. I push him over on his back. Even though he doesn't have an ounce of fat on him, he's dead weight. The dead word freaks me. I pinch his finger. It goes white before the blood rushes back to the surface. "Good. Breath and pulse. Hang in there, Gramps." I tilt his head back to give him maximum airflow through his trachea.

I move to his right side so I can watch the rise and fall of his chest, ready to do mouth-to-mouth if necessary. Sirens blare in the distance. Several heartbeats later, I hear a pounding on the door. "In here," I cry.

A tall woman and a thin balding man rush through the door, both wearing blue uniforms. They put oxygen on Gramps before they load him into the ambulance. I follow close behind in Beulah as we rush down the lane and onto the highway, their sirens blaring. The drive seems an eternity, but in reality we make good time.

They wheel Gramps into the emergency room. I'm left to fill out paperwork. From there they usher me to the waiting room where I drink several cups of bad-tasting coffee. The cool air chills my skin, adding to my discomfort. I shudder. Why are hospitals always so cold?

I look up from my contemplation of the design on the green and tan carpet to see Holly and Tyler rush in.

I carefully set the half-empty paper cup on the end table and push to my feet. Holly reaches me first. She grabs me and hugs me. "We just heard."

I look at Tyler over her head. He gives me a smile of so much love and compassion it confuses me. He wasn't speaking to me, we broke up and now when I need him…he's here. When Holly lets me go, he steps forward. I go rigid. He ignores it and puts his arms around me, drawing me close. "I'm so sorry, baby. So sorry."

"What exactly are you sorry for?" I ask stiffly.

"Everything," he whispers.

I'm not sure what everything encompasses, but I think he may be referring to this afternoon. "I can't think of anything but Gramps right now," I mumble against his chest.

"Of course." His hands move up and massage my tight shoulders.

"I'm scared," I whisper.

"He's going to be fine."

"You can't know that." I pull away from him.

"Your grandpa is a fighter. He's not going to let this beat him."

For a moment the thought bolsters me, before guilt I've held at bay floods my system. "I knew something was wrong. His color was bad and he was tired. I should have taken him to the doctor right away."

Holly grabs my hand and pulls me down to the industrial green settee in the waiting room. "Don't do this to yourself, Piper. This isn't your fault."

"Yes, it is," I insist. "I told him to call the doctor. I should have taken him myself." I pull my hands away and wring them.

Tyler moves in front of me, tugs me to my feet, and envelops me in his arms. I stand stiffly. But his lips against my hair and the softly whispered, "You aren't alone," is my undoing. I rest my head against his chest, taking in the comforting scents of soap, sun, and pine. Nothing has changed, but for the moment, I'll take the solace he offers. I take deep, shuddering breaths then force myself to step back.

He shifts his hands to my shoulders. "What can I do for you, Pip?"

Gramps' pet name for me. I shake my head and start to move away. His hands tighten just enough to hold me in place. "About this afternoon. I'm sorry. Can you forgive me? I was way out of line."

"I can't deal with this now."

"Of course, I understand. Just so you know that I'm here for you."

I nod, distracted. Doc Johnson steps into the waiting room. He is stooped with thinning white hair, his jacket rumpled. I rush toward him. "How is he?"

"He was lucky. He was hooked up to an electrocardiogram machine in the ambulance that was able to diagnose the severity of the attack. The paramedics phoned ahead to advise us of the situation."

"What was the severity?" I interrupt.

"No attack is good at his age, but as things go, it could have been a lot worse. In fact, I've moved him out of ICU."

"The electrocardiogram shows a small blockage that I think we can break down with drugs."

"But he passed out."

"He was dizzy and hit his head on the nightstand, knocked himself out."

"He's awake?"

Doc nods.

My muscles sag with relief.

"Knocking himself out might have been the best thing that happened to him. Allowed us to find that clot. Has your grandpa been under stress lately?"

Why would he be under stress just because he lives with a mutant? Guilt hits me hard. My shoulders slump. "He worries about me."

Doc gives me a pat on the shoulder. "Every parent or grandparent worries about their children. That's just part of the life cycle. Has he been working harder than usual, taking out extra tourist tours?"

I shake my head.

"I want him to take it easy, get plenty of rest. I'm going to give him nitrate tablets, but he's going to be okay. I want to keep him in the hospital for a couple of days to keep an eye on him."

"Of course."

"I'm going to put him on a daily aspirin. His blood pressure is a bit high. We'll put him on meds for that, too."

Poor Gramps, he hates meds. But he's going to take them. I'll make sure of that.

"I also want you to limit his cholesterol and fats and increase his fruits, vegetables, and whole grains."

"I'll take care of that."

"I know you will, honey." He pats me on the shoulder again. "Do you want to see him now?"

I nod eagerly. He escorts me to Gramps' room and leaves. I look down at the bed and a lump forms in my throat. Gramps is hooked to a heart monitor. Oxygen tubes run from his nose. An IV is stuck into his hand. He looks so frail.

I lean over and kiss his stubbly cheek. His eyes flutter open. I force my lips up. "Hi."

"Hi, honey." His voice is weak and raspy. "I hit my head. I'm losing my coordination in my old age."

I smile and carefully pick up his hand. "Did Doc tell you he found a small clot?"

"That old man overreacts," he grumbles, picking at his sheet with his free hand. "When can I get out of here?"

"Two days."

"Two days? I'm not staying here two days."

"Yes, you are. And when you get home, you are going to take it easy. And you're going to take the medication he's prescribed and follow the diet he recommends."

"Pip," he begins.

I cut him off. "Gramps, I can't lose you. You're all I have." I make a supreme effort. But tears leak out my eyes and fall on Gramps' hand.

"Don't cry, honey." His voice is gruff. "I'll do whatever you say. Don't worry. I plan on being around a good long time."

I sniff and wipe my eyes.

His head falls deeper into the pillow and his hand clasping mine goes slack.

"Get some rest, Gramps. I'll be right here."

"There's no need for you to stay. Go home. Do your homework, get some rest. Just do me a favor and don't go out in the ocean tonight, okay?"

Panic surges through my system. My dolphins. The research vessel. "Gramps..."

"Don't go out tonight, Pip. And go home. You need your rest." He tweaks at the sheet restlessly. His head shifts back and forth.

My head begins to pound. Everything is wrong. I need to check on the dolphins, but I won't lie to Gramps and I don't dare upset him. His state is so fragile. I want to stay but that would upset him, too. "Sure." I force a smile.

"Tyler can keep you company, but tell him to behave."

"Okay, Gramps." I see no point in telling him Tyler and I have broken up. I kiss him on the forehead. His skin feels frail and papery. "See you tomorrow."

"See you tomorrow." His eyes flutter shut.

When I step out, Tyler and Holly are waiting for me. "How is he?" Holly asks.

"He's going to be fine. He's just tired."

"Why don't you stay with us tonight?" Holly pushes her hair away from her face.

"That's a great idea," Tyler chimes in.

Not. "Thanks, but I'll be fine." I start toward the door.

"I'll see you home." Tyler falls into step beside me. Holly moves to my other side.

"Tyler, we're not an item anymore."

"What?" Holly grabs my arm and pulls me to a halt. "You guys haven't been going together long enough to break up."

"It was a misunderstanding," Tyler begins.

"No misunderstanding." I look at him before shoving through the door.

"Piper, wait up."

I keep going. Footsteps hurry behind me. I reach the truck and grab the handle. Tyler puts his hand on the door to keep me from opening it. I start to do a slow burn. Heat floods my face. "Get out of my way, Tyler."

He drops his hand. "I'm sorry. I was out of line today."

"It was a mistake from the beginning. I let my emotions override my common sense. You'll never accept me for who I am."

He opens my door and I climb inside.

"Who are you, Piper?" he asks quietly.

I don't bother to reply, just reach for the door to pull it shut.

He holds it open. "Whatever. I'll take Holly home then I'll be over."

"What part of breakup don't you understand?"

He leans in, his eyes sparking. I blink and start to draw back before catching myself. Instead, I straighten.

"I'm not leaving you alone after what happened last night. Deal with it."

Before I can protest, he slams my door and stalks away. I watch the stiff walk and straight line of his shoulders, a clear indicator he's pissed. Too bad, so am I.

Chapter 24

I gun my motor, probably waking any sleeping patients in the hospital and head home. I roll the window down and feel the cool breeze blow through the truck. I long for the ocean like a besotted woman longs for her lover. I need the water's silken caress. The energy and life under the water. The color and the wildness. I need it all.

And I'm worried about my dolphin friends. I don't want them killed so their body parts can be put in other human beings, turning them into something most would find unnatural, something like me.

I heave a sigh. I promised Gramps. So when I get home, instead of jumping in the ocean, I take a deep inhale of salt-laden air and head inside.

I'm munching on a Pop-Tart when Tyler arrives. The boy is fast, I'll give him that. A part of me is glad he's here. The part that would love to lie on the beach next to him, feel his warm skin under my fingertips, and his kissable lips pressed against mine in a wet, prolonged kiss. The rest of me is on guard, stressed to the max.

I crack the door and block entrance with my body. "This isn't necessary," I say ungraciously.

He's holding something behind his hand, but I smell it before he whips it in front of him. "I come bearing gifts." He looks pointedly at the Pop-Tart in my hand. "I didn't think you'd bother to eat."

How can he know me so well? Or maybe it's a teenage thing. On my list of Can't Resist are lattes and pizza. I step back and follow him into the kitchen.

He sets the brown box on the kitchen table, turns and just stares at me. I wipe my lip. Do I have crumbs on my mouth? "What?"

"In that getup you wear to school, it's easy to forget how beautiful you are."

"Please." I roll my eyes, ignoring the jump my stomach gives. It's the pizza, not the words, I tell myself. Or the sweetness of his smile. "I've got on knock-around clothes. How beautiful can I be?"

He takes a step closer. "Man, oh man, you make faded shorts and a pink top look like a fashion statement." He reaches to touch my hair, but I back away. "When I see you rise out of the water, it's like watching a mermaid come to life."

Mermaid, dolph-girl. I mentally shrug. "Tyler—"

"You don't need to say it. I know I screwed up with you, lost your trust. But I'm here for you, in any capacity that you want me. And I plan on sticking around."

I stare at him, my mind in turmoil. What's that supposed to mean? Would he be so willing to stay if he knew I'm a mutant? I almost ask, then control my unruly tongue. I guess I'll never know.

I break eye contact and shift away from the warm scent of male and sunshine. "Thanks for bringing the pizza. Want a soda?" I'm already heading for the fridge.

"Yeah, that would be great."

I pop the tabs on two cans of Coke and set them on the table. My chair scrapes as I sit down. The smells coming from the box are making my mouth water. I pull napkins out of the holder in lieu of plates.

Tyler reaches in, pulls out a piece, and demolishes it in three quick bites. He swallows and grins. I grin back. The awkwardness is broken, at least for now.

We eat in companionable silence. At least, I eat. Tyler inhales.

He glances out the window. "The sun is setting. Want to walk on the beach?"

Music to my ears. "I'd love to." I hop up, toss the pizza box in the trash, and hurry outside, Tyler right behind me. I head for the trail. Tyler takes my hand as we head down it, scuffing rocks and grabbing branches to keep from sliding.

We reach the bottom and gaze at the water. It laps lazily against the shore, creating hypnotic music. The spot we stand in is a secluded inlet. The sun is bright red and takes up the whole sky as it begins its descent into the water.

Tyler slips his arm around me. The moment is so perfect I lean against him. One or two premature stars are already in sight.

He places his lips gently on my brow before he draws me to him. It's been such a horrible day, first the breakup then Gramps. I can't help myself. I can't fight the attraction or the need for comfort. I turn into him, my hands clutching his shoulders, my fingers pressing through the fabric of his shirt, feeling the heat of his skin.

"Piper," he whispers before his mouth closes over mine. I blindly seek solace. I press against him as close as I can get. With a groan, he returns the pressure.

Whether it's the dolphin DNA or my human nature I have no desire or will to move away. My blood pulses a hot rhythm. I want more of him.

Somehow, we move to the ground. The sharp edges of small sandy pebbles poke through my clothes before Tyler rolls us over into a bank of wild grass and tiny flowers. A sweet scent rises around us as our bodies crush the flowers.

I pull his shirt over his head and feel smooth skin over ropy muscle beneath my fingers. His hands travel over me, leaving surges of electricity wherever he touches. His fingers come within inches of my blowhole, but I stay on my back, keeping it covered.

He shifts away from me, panting.

"Tyler?" I reach for him.

He heaves a long shuddering breath. "I can't believe I'm saying this, but we'd better stop."

Unfortunately, my response is all female. "You don't want me?" The words are out before I can stop them.

He gives a choked laugh, scooting away from me. "I think it's pretty obvious that's not the problem. In fact, I've never wanted anyone more." He shakes his head as if confused by the intensity. "Is this your way of saying we're a couple again?" He picks up a small stone and throws it toward the water, but we aren't close enough. The stone plops into the sand.

"No." I rub my arms, chilled, more alone than before.

A look of hurt crosses his face, but is quickly masked. "It's okay. It's my fault. I take responsibility."

"There's no fault involved." I sit up stiffly and pull down my top.

"I should clarify," he says gently. "My fault for the breakup. For this"—he gestures and grins—"I'm a guy. My only regret is stopping."

My confusion overcomes my embarrassment. "I don't understand."

He leans toward me, the grin gone, replaced with an intense expression. "I want you back. I want you to be my girl again. I was hit with a silly wave of insecurity when I said that stuff, something that normally doesn't happen to me." One side of his mouth goes up in a crooked smile.

He shifts and tugs at a blade of grass. "I don't make a habit of talking about this but I want you to understand. Remember when I told you my uncle is pretty high up in the Mafia?"

I nod, confused.

"My dad didn't share that information with my mom right away. When he did tell her, it caused a huge rift. It took over a year for them to mend their differences. Secrets aren't good, Piper."

"Why didn't your dad tell her?"

"He was afraid she wouldn't marry him." He shrugs. "It hit a nerve. Not to mention, the mystery is driving me wild."

I stare at the ocean. I can certainly relate to his dad, plus no matter how trustworthy Tyler is, I can't bring myself to share this particular secret. I heave a sigh of regret. A relationship isn't in my future. I'm destined to be alone.

A nagging little voice in my head says Gramps' family knew and kept mom's secret. Maybe not telling him is cowardice. But it's a risk I'm not willing to run.

"Tyler." The name comes out a squawk, possibly from the lump in my throat. I clear it and try again. "Tyler, it's not in the cards for me. I care about you, really care about you, but I can't be in a relationship right now."

I hunch my shoulders, waiting for his anger and hurt. Silence. I glance at him.

He touches my hand with the tips of his fingers. "I'm willing to wait. At some point you're going to decide you can't live without me and when you do, I'll be here."

He gives me his sweet crooked grin, the one that never fails to melt my heart. "You never react as I expect you to," I mutter.

"I've got to keep you on your toes. Are you ready to go back?" He gets up and pulls me to my feet.

I look longingly at the ocean. "I promised Gramps I wouldn't go out tonight. What if they've caught one? What if one of the dolphins is in trouble?" I bite my lip and fight against tears.

"Tomorrow, tell your gramps I'll go out with you."

"You'd do that for me?" I shake my head, trying to clear my thoughts, which are ricocheting against each other in confusion.

"You and the dolphins. We'll figure out who's behind this and put a stop to it."

The thought brings me up cold. A thousand emotions zing me. Of course, I want this thing stopped. But I'm not sure I want to get that close to who's responsible. I know in my bones it's the mutant lab.

And I don't want Tyler to find out about me. But that must come second to saving the dolphins.

He takes my hand and we head for the trail in silence. Halfway up it dawns on me, he never told me why he stopped tonight. We got tangled up in the secrets thing.

As if sensing my thoughts, something he seems able to do with alarming accuracy, he tugs on my hand, halting me as we enter the house. "I want to make love with you. I intend to." There comes that crooked grin. "But I don't want any regrets on your side. I'm afraid if it happened tonight there might be. You just haven't quite wrapped your head around the fact we belong together."

Would I have regretted it? My human side, maybe. My dolphin side, no. Dolphins are gregarious creatures without the inhibitions of humans.

I reach over and kiss his cheek. "You think too much. And it's not necessary for you to stay."

"Probably not. But I'm staying just the same."

"Stubborn." I shake my head and smile.

Except for the underlying sexual tension and the worry about my dolphins, the evening is comfortable, even fun. We settle in on the couch to do homework.

I look up from my laptop to find Tyler staring at me. "What?"

As if reading my thoughts, he says, "We should get the other kids involved in saving the dolphins."

"What do you mean?" I ask cautiously.

"Just make them aware. Lots of kids have boats, or their parents do. They could cruise the waters. In fact, let's take the boat out tomorrow evening."

"Has it been fixed yet?" I know it's been hauled in, but I'm not sure of the damages.

"No, but we could take my parents'."

"Or Gramps' old boat."

"Yeah."

I feel considerably cheered. Maybe there's something to this not flying solo stuff.

"It's a date."

I look at him uneasily.

"Figuratively speaking."

The evening passes quickly. At midnight, I make the couch up for Tyler then go to bed myself.

* * * *

The next morning when I get up Tyler's already gone. Before he left, he made coffee, bless him. The aroma lingers in the kitchen, so I know he hasn't been gone long. I dress quickly, grab a Pop-Tart and head for the hospital to take a quick peek at Gramps before I go to school.

I stick my head in the room. He's sleeping. I tiptoe over and study him. His color is good. The gray is gone from his skin. I hope it's not worry about me that landed him here.

As I leave the room, the nurse comes down the hall. "Little early for visiting," she comments.

"I wanted to check on him before I go to school."

"He's doing fine. He had a good night. I wouldn't be surprised if the doctor releases him."

Relief floods my system. "That's great news. I'll be back after school." I run for my truck and head for school.

I arrive with minutes to spare. As I push through the glass doors, Fahrenbacher steps away from the trophy case that lines the wall. "Hey, hot stuff."

I ignore him and keep walking. He falls in beside me, walking with a swagger. God's gift, etc. etc.

"What do you want, Fahrenbacher?" I boost my book bag higher on my shoulder and lengthen my stride, trying to get away from the asshole.

He keeps up with no apparent effort.

He leans toward me, invading my space. "You, sweet cheeks."

"Get over yourself."

"Leave that loser Carlisle and try a real man."

It's on the tip of my tongue to say Tyler and I are just friends, before sanity returns. The last thing I need is Fahrenbacher thinking he's got a clear field.

"Why don't you go out with me Friday night?"

"What do you want, Fahrenbacher?" Tyler shoulders his way between the two of us.

"I wasn't speaking to you, Carlisle." His swagger has stiffened, his manner belligerent.

I can almost smell the testosterone rolling off both of them.

"You're speaking to me now."

Fahrenbacher ignores him and says to me, "Think about it. I'll be in touch." He slams his shoulder against Tyler and strides away.

"That guy really gets on my nerves," Tyler mutters, watching Fahrenbacher disappear down the hall.

"Feeling seems to be mutual."

"What did he want?" His expression isn't quite a glare but close enough.

"Nothing important."

"What did he want, Piper?" His jaw clenches, his chin juts up.

I sigh in defeat. "He wanted a date."

"Are you going?"

"Are you insane? Forget Fahrenbacher. I certainly intend to."

As we slip into class, the bell rings. From the back row, Holly motions for me. She's saved two seats. Tyler and I sink down beside her.

She looks at Tyler and grins.

Tyler gives a small shake of his head. She frowns in confusion.

I slink down, hoping I won't be noticed. It's my lucky day. I'm not called on once. I should buy a lottery ticket.

The bell rings and I hurry to my next class. The day passes without incident. Sooner than I would have thought possible, the school day is done. I head for the hospital.

A glance in the rearview mirror shows Tyler right behind me. He catches my eye and lifts a hand. I wave back then concentrate on my driving.

When I pull into the parking lot, he parks next to me. We walk in together. Even though I know I shouldn't let it, his presence brings me comfort. I glance at him. He looks at me and gives a reassuring smile. I smile back.

He takes my hand. Reluctantly, I start to pull back. His grip tightens. He leans down close to my ear. "Friend." His breath sends shivers through me.

"Friend." I nod.

Doc Johnson is coming out of Gramps' room. He sees me and smiles. "Piper."

"How is he, Doc?"

"He's okay. We ran some more tests. Stress and an ECG. He didn't have a heart attack as I originally thought."

"He didn't? So he doesn't have a clot? How were they wrong about that?"

"He's suffering from angina. The symptoms are very similar. He had a small blockage; if the blockage had been complete it would have been a full-blown heart attack."

"I'm sorry, I still don't entirely understand."

"It's lack of blood and oxygen to the heart. It's treated pretty much the same as a heart attack. Nitrate tablets if needed and a change in his eating habits. If it doesn't get better we'll do an angioplasty but hopefully it won't come to that. Keep his stress level down."

I give a guilty start.

Tyler squeezes my hand.

"Can I take him home?"

"Yes, you may. Just remember what I said." He shoves his hands in his pockets and heads down the hall, his gait tired, his head and shoulders forward.

Two hours later the nurse is wheeling Gramps out of the hospital. Tyler insists on driving him home. I reluctantly agree. Beulah's shocks are shot.

I swing through Subway and pick Gramps up a turkey breast sub and apple slices, and meatball sandwiches with chips for Tyler and me.

When I get home, Tyler has already helped Gramps into his favorite recliner.

I fuss over him, draping an afghan around his lap.

"I'm not a damn invalid you know," he grumbles.

"I know." I hand him a paper plate with his sub and apple slices on it.

He looks at the turkey sub and apple slices on his plate, and the meatball sub and chips on mine and Tyler's, and raises his eyebrows.

"Doctor's orders."

"That old quack."

"Gramps."

He waves me off. "Have you stayed out of the ocean?"

"I said I would."

He studies me until I squirm uncomfortably. "It's hard on you."

"I'd be happy to go out with her, Mr. Dunn." Tyler volunteers.

He's probably wondering why it's hard on me.

Gramps brightens. "It would make me feel better. Asking Piper to stay out of the sea is like asking a greyhound not to run."

"It would be my pleasure." Tyler glances at me. "I spoke to several other students today. They're incensed that someone is hunting the dolphins. Do you know Anna Marie?"

"Vaguely."

She's organizing the students. The ones whose families have boats will patrol. Others will put up fliers and contact the local media. It'll take a few days to get everybody organized but hopefully it'll take care of the situation."

"That's wonderful. Thank you." I give him a warm smile. I can continue to keep an eye out without being visible. "I really appreciate it."

I glance over at Gramps. He's eaten half his sandwich and his eyelids are drooping. I take his plate. "Why don't you lay down, Gramps?"

"I think I will." He pulls himself out of the chair. "You and Tyler take your swim."

Swimming with Tyler is tricky. But I'm so anxious to get in the water, I'm willing to deal with it.

"My trunks are in the car. I'll get them and change." Tyler rises.

"Be careful, Pip." Gramps pats me awkwardly on the shoulder and shuffles to his room. I go to mine and step out of my clothes. As usual, I've got on a two-piece in place of underwear. Some girls collect shoes. I collect swimsuits. I have a couple dozen. The one I've got on is pink with black polka dots.

I walk out and Tyler is standing in the living room, his trunks hooked on one finger. He looks at me and his eyes cross. Heat floods my face. I point down the hall. "You can change in the bathroom."

He nods. A slow appreciative smile crosses his features, his gaze travels from my head to my toes and back again. "Nice swimsuit." He strolls away whistling.

When he comes out, he's in gray, knee-length trunks with a green drawstring and large pockets. I glance at him unobtrusively, taking in his long lean body, the flat stomach, and ropy muscles.

He catches me looking and teases. "No touching the merchandise. We're just friends, remember?"

I glance away.

He chuckles. "And as your friend, let me say, you look damn hot. Not that I notice."

I roll my eyes. How I'm going to keep him in line is beyond me. We leave the house and stroll down the path to the water. I try not to remember what happened the last time we were here. Of course, it's the only thing I think about.

I look anywhere but at Tyler's face. Glancing down, I notice the bulge in his pocket. "What's that?" I point then feel myself blush, hoping he doesn't misunderstand and think I'm making sexual innuendos.

If he does, he doesn't say anything. Instead, he reaches in his pocket and pulls out an underwater camera. "In case you want to swim out further or get too far ahead of me, I can keep an eye on you."

Never known for thinking on my feet, all I can think to say is, "Oh." I hold out my hand.

"It's a digital with night vision. If we see the ship, I might be able to get some pics."

"What a great idea."

"Thanks." He hooks it around his neck. "Ready?"

"Ready."

We wade into the water. The cool slapping liquid is in direct contrast to the warm humid air on our shoulders. When the water hits my waist, I begin to swim, Tyler follows suit.

I flip onto my back and watch him. He has a strong sure stroke. I roll into a ball, like an otter playing, before I stretch out and swim. Tyler stays at my side matching me stroke for stroke. I could outswim him but have no desire to.

A few moments later, something wet and slick pushes us apart.

"Hey." Tyler looks around wildly. I laugh.

The dolphin pulls ahead of us, lifts his head out of the water and chatters.

"How cool is that? Though, he nearly gave me a heart attack." Tyler dog paddles and pushes water out of his face. "Does this happen to you often?"

"Yeah," I admit.

"You're an amazing girl."

Two more dolphins join us. Tyler takes out his camera and starts shooting. When he turns his camera in my direction, I hold up my hand. "None of me."

He opens his mouth then nods. "Okay. How about you take one of me with our friends here?"

I take the camera and as I click, one of them jumps in the air and comes down with a splash that drenches us.

We laugh. I hand him back his camera.

Suddenly, Tyler stiffens and points. The dolphins grow quiet. In the distance is the shadowy outline of a boat.

Paddling with his feet, Tyler raises his camera, focuses and starts shooting.

"Let me see." I hold out my hand and he hands me the camera. The view is distorted. I blink, wipe the water out of my eyes, and focus. The boat is dark and nondescript, not easily recognizable, but what isn't are the two divers looking over the side.

Chapter 25

"It's the same boat, Tyler." The water ripples around us as we paddle in place.

"Are you sure?"

"Of course not," I snap. "I'm going closer." I move forward.

"Wait."

"What?" My mind is already on getting closer to the boat, diving down and seeing if they have any unsuspecting dolphins in tow.

"These guys are dangerous."

"I'll be careful. I've got to see if they've captured any dolphins."

The gray waves lap around us. The moon shines down, making the sea sparkle. It outlines the boat and the figures on it. I wonder uneasily if they can see us. I'm used to swimming underwater, not on the surface.

"Okay, let's go."

I look at him. "I'll be swimming underwater."

"I can swim underwater."

"I'm sure you can, but not for the length of time I'll be down."

"How can you stay underwater?"

"Not now."

"Then I'll swim on top."

"No, they might see you. Just stay where you are and keep an eye on things."

"I'm not letting you ."

We both know it's an empty threat.

"At least stay near, until I get closer."

"Okay." I nod reluctantly. We swim forward another hundred yards, then another. The murky outline of the craft becomes more distinct.

I motion Tyler to stop. I drop my voice to a whisper. Sound carries on the wind. "Better not go any further."

He touches my arm, his voice low and urgent. "I don't have scuba gear. I can't go down and help you if you get in trouble."

"Who's going to get in trouble?"

"Famous last words."

"If I see anyone, I'll swim for the surface. Okay?"

"Promise?"

"I promise."

"Be careful." He kisses me quick and hard, his lips cold and salty.

"Always." I curve my body to drop down into the sea.

Tyler grabs my arms. His grip slips but he holds on.

"How long can you stay under water?"

"Half an hour."

"Half an hour?" His jaw drops.

"Don't say a word."

"Half…"

I put a finger to his lips. "Not a word."

"All right, all right not a word, but if you aren't back in half an hour, I'm coming looking for you."

"Whatever," I mumble under my breath before I drop into the ocean. I go deeper into the murky dark. I blink several times, my eyes adjusting to the black. Stretching out my arms and kicking, I swim toward the boat. I should have given Tyler Gramps' distress watch.

Oh well, if something goes wrong, I can at least contact Gramps. But it would have to be an emergency. Gramps' heart can't take the stress.

A school of small, gray fish swim close by until they notice me and dart in a different direction.

Next to the boat, a young dolphin is caught in the trap. I swim closer. He doesn't look good. How long has he been here? His color is off. The eyes have a dull, glazed look instead of the bright lively intelligence that normally shines through them.

I draw closer. He either recognizes my dolphin DNA or still has an innate trust of humans. His tail does a short wag like a dog's.

"There, there," I coo into the water, bubbles spewing out of my mouth.

I pry open the door.

He flashes by then comes back and shoves me hard. A warning. A second later, I'm grabbed and pushed into the cage. The dolphin darts around chattering.

Before whoever is behind me can shut the door, I grab the sides and kick at it. I push backward. Someone grabs my thighs and shoves me forward.

I twist out of his grasp, kick straight back, catching my attacker in the stomach. Frantically, I propel myself backward, my legs free. Freedom is close. I've nearly wiggled out of the pen when another set of hands grabs my left thigh. I kick out with my other foot and catch him in the jaw. He lets go. I drop lower. I'm almost free when he grabs my arm. I ball my fist. Before I can strike, his fingers bite into a nerve. I cry out, bubbles pouring out of my mouth.

My arm is momentarily numb. I strike out with my other. He brings the side of his hand down on my shoulder. Both of my arms are now useless. The numbness will fade, but will it be soon enough?

I draw my knees up to my chin, ready to kick out. By now the other man has recovered. They both dive at me. I make one last desperate kick. One grabs my feet, the other my legs and they push me into the cage and swiftly lock the door.

One motions toward the surface. They swim to the ladder alongside the boat and pull themselves up, leaving me to drown in the cage.

Chapter 26

Oh my God. How much time do I have left? Twenty minutes?

I frantically punch the button on my watch. Not that it will do any good. Gramps can't possibly get here in time. He'll freak. But if I don't press it and disappear, he'll do worse than freak. Stress either way.

Tyler! No. Tyler can't reach me, he's too far away.

Are they seriously going to leave me trapped here to die? For freeing a few dolphins? What kind of monsters are these people anyway? My heart pounds. I'm on the verge of hyperventilating. I push frantically at the bars. Maybe I can work the lock from the inside. I stretch my hand out. No, I can't reach it.

The cage lurches. I clutch the bars.

It's being hauled up. The cage breaks through the water and I'm dangling over the boat, breathing hard. I chuff. Water powers out my blowhole. I hope it's unnoticed in the streams of water pouring off me. "Tyler!" I scream.

The cage rocking, the divers lower it to the floor of the boat. *Thump.* I feel the jar from the soles of my feet to the top of my head. Panicked, I breathe in short, sharp spurts. Fear rips through me. I try to pull myself together, afraid I'll pass out. *Oh God.*

"What are you doing?" My voice is raw with terror. My worst fear in the world is being realized.

They don't answer. Instead, the man closest to me turns and asks, "You called out a name. Is someone with you?"

I stare at him defiantly. No easy feat, since I'm trembling like a leaf.

"We better get out of here," he says to his partner. The man with him disappears below and the boat starts moving through the water. It picks up momentum. For a craft its size, it's moving quickly.

"Help!" I clutch the bars and try to rattle them. I think I hear a muffled cry further out, but it's drowned out by the boat.

My shoulders sag. Even if Tyler saw me in the cage through the camera, now the boat's moving he can't possibly get to me in time. Better if he doesn't try. The boy would drown. And Gramps can't possibly get to me either. My only hope is he can follow the GPS signals.

I scream loud and long. When I stop for breath, I hear sounds from the deep. A whale responds. Dolphins chatter. The sounds are faint. It's hard to hear below the sea when I'm above it.

A diver rushes toward me, grabs my arm, and swings me out of the cage. The feeling is back in my arms and shoulder. I put my fists up. Before I can get in a fighting stance, he gets me in a crushing lock. There's no doubt this man knows more about martial arts than I.

"Where are you taking me?" I manage to gasp over the restrictive pressure on my neck.

He doesn't respond. His face gleams white against the dark. I'm sure I can see him more clearly than he can see me. The boat is running without lights.

He drags me below and tosses me in a small room that has a large tank filled with water against the far wall.

"Since you like to swim so much, maybe we should just toss you in the tank, water girl." He laughs, then shuts and locks the door.

I pound on it. "Let me out."

"What are the chances of that happening?" He laughs again.

His footfalls grow fainter as he trots up the stairs.

Yelling and cursing, I beat my fists against the door till they're raw and bleeding. No one's coming. I close my eyes, sag against it, and sink to the floor. I wait for my eyes to adjust to the dark and look around.

The sight of the water tank sends acid spurting through my stomach. How many of my aquatic brothers and sisters have been captured and used for unimaginable experiments?

Could these divers be working for the same people who experimented on my mom?

My head tells me it could be any number of people who are after the dolphins. Unscrupulous people who want to make a quick buck, maybe sell them to foreign marinas. My heart tells me it's the same evil group that captured and did unspeakable things to my mother.

My breath comes out in a harsh sigh. Fear and misery permeate the room, leaving a sick smell of despair. For a moment, it coats my skin like dark oil. I feel helpless and alone. I curl into a ball and rock back and forth.

I don't know how much time passes. Finally, I take a deep breath, exhale, and straighten my shoulders. I can't give in to the feeling of hopelessness that engulfs me.

I try to think of a plan. I'm on my own. Gramps can't call the police or coast guard. What would he say, "I need help, someone's abducted my mutant granddaughter?"

I swallow hard. The authorities would inevitably lead to the government. All roads lead to an experimental lab.

I can only hope Tyler will report to my grandfather, not head for the police or coast guard.

I take a shuddering breath as I face the inevitable. I'm alone. I come from strong stock, I tell myself. I can and will survive. And I will find a way back home. I fight back the voice screaming in my head. *I can't survive this. I can't. I can't.*

I hear footsteps. Two sets. I flatten my back against the wall behind the door. I flex my knees and fist my hands, forcing back the trembles.

When they step through the door, I leap and kick out. I catch the closest in the thigh. He crumbles. The other flips on the light, temporarily blinding me. "Nice kick, kid, but I wouldn't."

Blinking rapidly, trying to see, I whirl toward him ready to kick out. The gun in his hand stops me cold.

"I'm not sure that's such a good idea, Joe." The other man picks himself off the floor. They've both changed into black jeans and black shirts. They've made no attempt to hide their faces, which doesn't exactly make me feel all warm and cozy.

"You got any better ideas? How many times has she managed to escape? I don't want to tell the boss we've failed again. Do you?" He doesn't wait for an answer but points and fires.

I stiffen, waiting for the bullet to rip through me. All I feel is an annoying prick when the dart pierces my skin…then nothing.

Chapter 27

My head is muzzy, like it's wrapped in cotton, my skin clammy. I sniff, expecting the smell of Gramps' coffee. Instead, I smell sterility and antiseptic. Something dark and horrible shifts in the back of my brain. I sniff again, nothing, no stale food smells, no dirty clothes, no sunshine, no sea air.

I try to blink my eyes open but they're pasty with sleep. I reach to rub them and discover my hands are strapped down. *Oh My God.* Memory hurtles back. Terror takes over.

I squeeze hard until I can pry my eyes partially open and squint. I lift my head to look around. When I'm extremely upset, my legs tingle. They're tingling now.

I'm in a hospital gown strapped to a bed. The walls are pristine white, the floor white marble. There's not so much as a speck of dust or dirt.

Dread slides up my spine like a slithering snake. It leaves me cold and shaken. I can't stand it. I have to get out of here. I yank at my restraints. Then stiffen…someone's coming.

The door glides soundlessly open. I smell him before I see him, spicy aftershave and sea air. No, not sea air…dolphin.

Dolphins have little to no scent. They don't have skin glands so they don't sweat. But to me they have their own special tang, a mix of sea salt and coral. The best smell in the world. Coral has a floral fruity scent with a wisp of salt.

I look up expectantly. When I see him, my breath catches and my heart stops. If it didn't already belong to Tyler, I would lay it forever and irrevocably at this boy's feet.

To look at him no one would ever know. He looks like he's just stepped off one of California's beaches, surfboard in hand. His hair is thick and streaked the color of wheat, his body lean and tanned. But I know. Feel it in every fiber of my being. A kindred spirit. *A dolph.*

"Hello." His masculine voice is melodious, like mine. There's one other giveaway. His eyes are turquoise. For a moment, I forget the terror that weakens my bowels. Underneath the fear, I feel a tiny spurt of happiness. I'm not alone in the universe.

"Hello." I do nothing to disguise my voice. With him, there's no reason.

He gives me a slow smile that stretches across his face and reaches his beautiful eyes. I've never thought of my own as being beautiful, more of a nuisance. After looking at his, I might have to reevaluate.

"Where am I?"

"Why have they strapped you down?" he asks at the same time. Both of us laugh. Given the circumstances, it's unbelievable that I can laugh at all.

Before either of us can respond, the door opens again. A silver-haired man of indeterminate age steps in. He wears a crisp white lab coat and has a stethoscope slung round his neck. His scent is as sterile as the room; his face holds no expression. His lips are thin, almost reptilian. My skin crawls and I push against the mattress.

"Joel." The doctor turns toward the dolph-boy.

At least I now know his name.

"Dr. Stranger." He nods.

"I see you discovered our guest."

"Yes." He smiles at me then looks at the doctor. "Why is she in restraints?"

The doctor appears surprised at the question. "I deemed it necessary."

"But…"

Dr. Stranger interrupts. "Joel, leave us for a bit. You can show our guest around the premises later. Right now I need to examine her."

Conflict flickers across Joel's features. He obviously doesn't want to leave me nor does he want to stay for a physical exam that could be an embarrassment to us both.

"I won't hurt her and I promise I'll remove the restraints. You can show her around after lunch."

Joel nods. He gives me a reassuring smile and a promise. "I'll be back."

As soon as the door shuts, the doctor pulls out a key and unlocks a small white cabinet on the far wall. He pulls out a needle and syringe, looks at it, and flicks it with his finger.

"What is that?" My body stiffens. My muscles tense. If I could figure out a way, I'd fight.

"Just something to help you relax. You want those restraints off, don't you?"

"You can't do that without shooting me up?" I turn my head as far to the side as I can get it and still keep an eye on that needle.

"It's for your own good. Trust me."

"Right." Like I've never heard that one before.

He swabs my arm. The scent of alcohol sickens me. He sticks my arm with the needle. I barely feel the prick. What I do feel is the medication traveling through my veins, relaxing my body as it moves through it, making it heavy. I try to fight it but a strange lethargy takes possession of me.

"I'm going to remove your restraints." He unbuckles the arm bands.

I try to gather myself for flight, but I can't seem to pull myself together, uncoordinated as a rag doll. A remote portion of my brain that the drug either hasn't reached or can't is shrieking. *Fight!* The medication doesn't touch the fear. The fear is still there. I can't remember a time I've been this terrified of anything. It's so strong, I swear I could choke on it.

"Why don't you shower? I'll have the nurse lay out some clothes for you, then bring you to my office. I'll answer any questions you have. After that someone will show you to your room."

I don't respond, just stare straight ahead. After he leaves, I push off the bed. I grab the frame to keep from crumpling. Maybe the shower will help me shake off the effects of this drug and I can get out of here.

I step into the bathroom. It's spacious but sterile like the other room. I let the sack-shaped, limp hospital gown fall to the floor. I reach to unfasten my distress watch and realize for the first time, it's gone.

A single tear slips out and trails down my cheek as I grasp the fact I've lost the last connection to my grandfather. I can only hope by the time they discovered it, Gramps had my location. Holding that thought like a lifeline, I step carefully into the warm spray. Along with the water comes a light, floral aroma. The water must trigger a valve that releases the scent. The combination soothes and falls on my skin like spring rain.

I stand beneath the warm wet beads, my hands against the wall. The needles of water from the jets massage my body, making it tingle. For a few blissful moments, the fear of being strapped to a table and cut on recedes. Not altogether, but enough where I can function.

I step out, towel dry my hair, and with clumsy steps move into the adjoining room.

Clothes are laid out on the bed: a white, short-sleeved silk blouse and tan khaki shorts. A little preppie for my taste but that's the least of my concerns. The shower offset some of the sluggishness the drug caused, unfortunately not enough for me to make a run for it. Awkwardly, I get dressed.

My stomach rumbles. It's been a while since I ate. I'm not even sure what time it is.

I wonder if the door is locked. I get up and walk toward it.

As if on cue, a perky young woman comes through it. She's dressed in a traditional white nurse's uniform that rustles when she walks. She looks fresh out of college, with curly, shoulder-length auburn hair. She's not at all what I expect of someone who cuts into people's brains for a living.

Smiling, she walks toward me, her hand outstretched. "I'm your nurse. My name is Casey."

I back away. I don't trust her. I can't trust anyone in this Godforsaken place, except perhaps the dolph-boy, my kindred spirit.

She stops and smiles encouragingly. "I won't hurt you."

"You're my nurse?"

"Um-hm. I've come to take you to Dr. Stranger's office." She opens the door and waits for me. I stare at her, frozen in place. Are they going to cut on me?

"Come on, dear."

I weigh my options. Better to walk out under my own steam than be hit with more drugs and end up in his office anyway.

I'm wearing a pair of tan Tirra sandals that were left by the bed. The rubber soles muffle the sound as we walk across the white marble floor. To be more accurate, Casey walks. I shuffle along like an old woman.

I glance from side to side looking for exits. Where are the guards? Where is security? Does he keep personnel at a minimum because of the experiments? As we walk, I see the tiny red glow of security cameras along the hall. Security may not be visible, but someone is watching somewhere.

We turn down a hall and the white marble gives way to lush white carpet. The walls are no longer white but a soft powder blue. Peaceful seascapes hang on the wall. To my inexperienced eye, they look expensive.

With each step, I become more nervous. A fine sheen of perspiration beads on my forehead. If it weren't for my feet feeling like they're encased in cement, I'd make a break for it, even if it's one of the stupidest things I could do right now. The truth is I'm scared spitless.

"Where are we?" I ask, as much for information as to keep the fear at bay over what awaits me.

"In a private clinic. A very nice one."

"Where is this nice private clinic located?"

"I'm not sure."

"Really?" How can she not know? She works here.

"Because the nature of the doctor's work is top secret, we are flown in and out. I know it's on an island." She smiles brightly. "I live here most of the time. When I want to take vacation or visit my family, I'm flown home. One word of indiscretion, I'd be fired without a reference."

"You're okay with that?"

"Sure. It's only for a couple of years and then I'll retire."

Huh. The pay must be very good indeed.

"It's like being in the air force or peace corps." She giggles. She stops at a thick set of double doors and knocks.

"Come in."

We step into a richly appointed office. Everything is dark wood and leather, a masculine room. The doctor sits behind a large mahogany desk.

A wide window is on the far wall. I swear I can smell salt water through the glass. It draws me. With a shambling gait, I walk toward it. We are on a bluff that overlooks the sea. I breathe deep and long, trying to gain strength from the waves below for whatever is to come.

"Thank you, Casey. That will be all."

"Yes, doctor." Her bubbly personality is subdued.

He waits for her to leave then leans back in a black leather chair, which sighs with his movements. He motions to a matching chair across from the desk. "Won't you sit down?"

I straighten my shoulders. I will not show fear, though it's almost impossible to hide the tremors running through me. I bite my lip and shuffle to the chair where I sit on the edge of the buttery-soft leather.

He steeples his fingers and studies me, his manner clinical. "What's your name?"

"Piper." My voice is strained. I clasp my hands to stop the tremors.

"Piper what?"

"Just Piper." I don't want this monster to have any connection to my grandfather.

"We'll let that go for now. I examined you while you slept. I also drew some blood. Your DNA is very interesting."

I feel violated. The idea of him touching me makes me nauseous. "Would I be correct in assuming you are ultimately responsible for it?" I try to keep the loathing out of my voice. The answer is important.

"Why would you think that?"

"Joel. He's like me, isn't he?"

He seems pleased with my response. "You're a perceptive young woman."

I shift on the chair and the expensive leather whispers. I'd like to buy Gramps a recliner made of this stuff. The thought brings me up short. Will I ever see my Gramps again? Has my disappearance set him back? Is he in the hospital? Pain washes through me. I clamp it down. I don't want this monster to see it. He would find a way to use it against me.

He leans back in his chair, still studying me. "I started my research when I was a young man. With the right investors, it's proved quite profitable."

I interrupt. "Are there many like me?"

"No, not many. But the few that exist have made me millions.

"One of my finest creations, along with her keepers, was lost at sea during a terrible storm. Or so I thought. You carry her DNA. You are very like her. How fortuitous for me you were determined to free my dolphins."

Chapter 28

His finest creation...he's referring to my mom. This is the man who turned my beautiful mother into a lab rat and made her life a living hell. Is he responsible for her death as well? Had he found her, chased her, trying to get her back? I want to beat my fists against his chest, shred his expressionless face with my nails, and shriek at the top of my lungs. I lunge to my feet.

He studies me coolly. "I can inject you with drugs that will put you into a permanent coma and still harvest your body parts. Now be a good girl and sit down."

I stand clenching and unclenching my hands. Reluctantly, I sink back in the chair. Instead of ripping his eyes out, I ask, "What do you mean *your* dolphins?"

"I have found the dolphins off the California coast have the best temperaments for my experiments."

My stomach rolls: first my mom, now my poor dolphins. He killed my father, too. I can't prove it, but deep inside I know it.

He takes off his glasses and cleans them, inspects the lens, then puts them back on. "Sacrifices must be made for science."

"Science or money?" *Bastard.*

"Often the two go hand in hand."

"Lucky for you."

"Yes, isn't it?"

"What do you intend to do with me?"

He taps his fingertips. "Since your mother took the mixing of dolphin blood and human blood to the next level, I'd be curious to see the results of a third generation."

Ice chills my blood. "You plan to use me as a brood mare?"

"Nothing so plebian, I assure you. You are a miracle of science. I want you to be part of creating another miracle."

What exactly does this madman have in mind? Surely, he's not thinking about Joel. Is he?

"What if I say no?"

He doesn't even dignify that with a response. Instead, he glances at his watch. "I'm going to have Casey show you to your room. We can talk more later." He pulls out his phone and speed dials. "Casey, Piper is ready to go to her room."

I looked at the phone. "Can I call my grandfather?"

"There will be no contact with the outside world. This is your home now. I trust you'll find it pleasant."

My home? My home is with Gramps. The ocean. But not this house of horrors. My God what if I find myself strapped to a table and a fin added behind my blowhole? My stomach heaves. I feel sick. Bile rises in my throat. It takes every ounce of willpower I possess to keep from throwing up.

A knock sounds at the door.

"Come in."

Casey opens the door. I push up from the chair. I've got to get out of here.

"Send a tray to her room. After she's eaten, have Joel show her around the facilities."

"Yes, sir."

She smiles at me. I follow her out the door and fall in step beside her. The drug that makes me feel encased in cement is wearing off. We walk to the elevator and step in. Casey pushes the button for four and we glide up.

Should I try to overpower her? A security camera is in the upper corner of the elevator. No good.

The door opens and we're in a large suite. In the center is a big screen TV that rivals any theatre I've been in, along with a game station, stereo and a cappuccino machine. A table sits in the corner, next to a fridge and microwave. A middle-aged woman dressed in a blue uniform is stocking the refrigerator. She smiles and nods when we walk by. If she's carrying a weapon, it's concealed.

The lounge is larger than our cottage back home. There are three doors on each side. Casey heads for the furthest on the left. She opens the door and motions me in.

The room is a combination bedroom-sitting room, the bedroom set back in a large alcove. The walls are a pale coral, and a pink and coral duvet covers the queen-size bed. A painting of a sunset done in pinks, red, and coral draws the eye to the far wall. But what catches and holds my gaze is the view.

It's similar to the one on the second floor, all craggy rocks and ocean below. It draws me. I walk to the window and give myself to the pull of the sea. How long will it be before I feel the silken caress of waves against my skin, like the beckoning arms of one's beloved?

"How do you like it?"

"It's fine." For a prison.

"Is there anything you need?"

A way out of here. I shake my head. She sounds more like a social secretary than a nurse, but I don't doubt she works effectively in either capacity.

"Are you hungry?"

On cue, my stomach juices start rolling in my tummy.

She points at an intercom on the wall. "Just press the button and talk into the intercom. Order whatever you like."

"Anything?"

"Pretty much. I'll just check your vitals before I go."

"Is that necessary?"

"Probably not. But it's my job." She checks my pulse, blood pressure and takes my temperature.

"Everything is great. Your blood pressure is a little high but since you're in new surroundings, it's nothing to worry about."

New surroundings sounds much more socially acceptable than kidnapped.

She walks to the door, turns, and smiles. "If you need me, just call me on the intercom. Okay?"

"Okay."

The door swings silently shut behind her. I hurry to the door and crack it open. Casey is gone, but the woman who was filling the refrigerator lounges in a nearby chair reading a magazine. It's then I notice the Taser on her hip. I let the door close.

I walk around the room. No escape exits except through the door. I also look for a security camera but don't see one in the room. It's either well hidden or I've caught a break.

The hollow feeling in my stomach is more than just nerves. When was the last time I ate? *With Gramps.* My knees give. I grab the edge of the sofa. Hopelessness overwhelms me. I take a deep breath, then another and another. Finally, my fight comes back along with my spine. Gramps didn't raise a quitter. I will get out of here. In the meantime, I need to keep my strength up. Determined, I stride to the intercom and press the button.

"How may I help you?" The tinny voice echoes from the intercom.

"I'd like lunch."

"What would you like?"

Talking to the wall is odd, even for me. I persevere. "I'd like a hamburger, fries, and a mocha latte."

"Okay, it will be around twenty minutes."

"Thank you." I click off and take a closer look at the room. There's a pretty little white desk with a laptop and a bookshelf over it. I run a finger over the titles: thrillers, YAs, and philosophy.

I sink down in the chair. Does the computer have Internet hookup? I open the cover, nothing but games, Word, and Excel. I hadn't expected anything. That would have been too easy.

A few minutes later, there's a knock on the door. A woman with graying hair scraped back from her face walks in and sets a tray in front of me. The smell makes my mouth water. I bite into the burger hungrily. I take a healthy sip of my latte. I swear it's the best I've ever had.

I clean my plate in an embarrassingly short time. I'm crunching on the last, still-hot fry when someone knocks on my door again.

I jump up, prepared to run, though I have no idea where. "Who is it?"

The door opens. I let out my held breath and relax. Joel stands in the doorway, smiling, a young girl beside him. I can't decide who's prettier: him or Tyler. They both take my breath away.

"Hi, Piper."

"Hi, Joel." I know I'm wearing a goofy grin, but that's okay. He is, too.

The young girl is hanging back. He pulls her forward. "Piper, this is Amy. Amy, Piper."

"Hi." She smiles shyly.

"Hi."

"Joel says you're like us." She takes a hesitant step into the room. She's a beauty with shiny straight black hair, olive skin and…turquoise eyes. She has the melodious voice of a dolph.

I point at my eyes and nod. "Come in and sit down." I motion toward the cream-colored leather couch against the wall.

Amy sinks down, draws her legs together, and hunches her shoulders. Joel sprawls out.

Chewing on her lip, Amy glances down.

I have so many questions. I should be trying to figure a way to get out of here, but there's so much I want to know. To be able to talk to another dolph, someone I didn't even realize existed. It's like thinking you're the last person on earth and discovering you're not. It's almost worth being captured, almost. "Do either of you have any dolphin characteristics? Besides the turquoise eyes and lyrical voice that seems to be unique to dolphs?"

She looks at Joel questioningly. He bends his head toward her and nods.

"I have stereoscopic vision. I can see well in water or on land." She clears her throat, self-consciously. "Where I'm different is in the dark, or at night, a layer that glows comes down over my eyes. In bright light, I have a brownish filter over my irises, kind of like wearing contacts."

"Wow." I lean forward, enthralled. "Can I see?"

She looks around. "Do you have a flashlight you can shine in my eyes?"

"I have no idea."

"Check your nightstand. There's probably one in there for emergencies." Joel chimes in.

I do as he says. Sure enough, there's a small penlight. I flip it on. For a small light, it's powerful.

"Are you sure you don't mind me shining this in your eyes?"

She laughs. "It's okay."

I grimace then shine it at her left eye. As I watch, a brown filter comes down like a shade and covers the iris. "Cool." I whoop. "Anything else?"

She points in the direction of her sandals. For the first time I notice her feet. "They're webbed. Amazing."

"It doesn't bother you?"

"Bother me? To find I'm not alone in the universe? You've got to be kidding."

I turn to Joel. "Your turn for show and tell."

"I am an extremely fast swimmer and I can leap in the air like a dolphin when I swim."

I lift back and forth on my toes and nod. "Anything else?"

"Isn't that enough?" He gives me a slow wicked grin.

My knees grow weak and the pit of my stomach goes soft. What's wrong with me? I'm in love with Tyler. I shake my head.

"Well then, Miss Greedy, I can detect chemicals in the water with my taste buds."

I twist my head to the side and study him; my eyes narrow thoughtfully.

As if reading my mind, he nods. "Exactly. Oil slicks, chemical spills." He shrugs. "I'm worth mega bucks."

"What do you mean?" Goose bumps stand up on my arms. I rub them.

"We're bred or created, as the case may be, to be sold."

For a moment, I'm speechless. I don't know which appalls me more, what he says or the matter-of-fact manner he says it in.

"Doesn't that bother you?" I demand.

"What's the point? It is what it is."

I start to protest. His mouth thins and his eyes narrow. I swallow what I'm about to say and ask instead, "How long have you been here?"

"As long as I can remember." He crosses his legs at the ankles. He looks comfortable, at ease.

I turn to Amy. "You?"

"Since I was born."

"You were born here?" I shift on the hard chair.

"Yeah. Our mother was a lab rat. She was artificially inseminated with human sperm and her germ line altered with dolphin DNA. "

"Oh." What can I possibly say? "How old are you?"

"Fifteen."

What she said dawns on me. "Our mother?"

"Joel is my brother."

I look at Joel. He nods.

"Is your mother here?" I dance my fingers along the desk.

"She died having me. They think it was something in the Dolphin DNA that her body was trying to reject."

"I'm sorry." My blood roars through me, first hot, then cold. How can they live here? Live with people that killed their mother? Joel looks out the window. A shadow crosses his features. Amy's shiny hair drops across her face as she lowers her head. Who am I to judge?

Joel clears his throat and looks at me. His smile looks forced. "We showed you ours. Now you show us yours." He wiggles his eyebrows.

I laugh. "All right." I rise, walk over to them, turn around, and pull the back of my shirt up.

The sofa sighs as they push up. They stand close to me. I can feel Joel's warm breath on my shoulder blade. It makes me shiver.

He's the first to notice. "Oh my God, an honest to God blowhole." His voice is filled with excitement.

"Where? Where? Let me see." Amy forgets her shyness and hops around me.

Joel places a warm finger just below my blowhole. Nerves ripple under my skin. His finger slowly traces circles down my back before he removes his hand.

"That is so cool." Amy's voice is filled with awe. Light as a butterfly, she touches it.

When she removes her hand, I pull down my shirt.

"Has anyone ever seen it?" she asks.

"Outside of my immediate family you're the first. Since it's between my upper shoulder blades, my hair hides it. But if I'm feeling particularly paranoid I punch holes in one of those round bandages and cover it. That way if anyone asks, I tell them I've scratched the mole on my back."

They laugh.

"I get webbed-toes and you get a blowhole. It's so not fair," Amy complains.

Commiserating, I pat her shoulder. I feel at home with them. Dolph-children like me. It fills an empty space deep inside me.

"Come on and we'll show you around." Joel motions me toward the door. Amy tags behind.

"Are there any more of us?" I ask as we walk through the lounge and head down the hall to the elevator.

"Not at the moment." Joel punches the button for the first floor.

It glides down. The door opens. A middle-aged man with a shock of red hair, wearing a guard's uniform, sits at a desk with security screens behind him. There must be at least twenty videos running. I'm mildly relieved to see there're no pictures of my bedroom. "Hello Amy, Joel."

"Hello, Ed." Amy says.

"Ed." Joel nods.

They hold out their arms and a scanner is run over them.

He looks at me. "And who might you be?"

"This is Piper," Joel responds before I can say anything. "She's one of us." He turns to me. "Have you been chipped?"

"What?"

"No, she'll need a wristband," he tells the guard. The guard studies my turquoise eyes and nods. He pulls out a band, activates it, and slides it onto my wrist.

"It has a tracking device in it," Amy explains.

Fury floods my system. "A freaking tracker. What am I, a damn dog?"

"Piper." There's warning in Joel's voice.

Amy's head is down, her face red. They've chipped her, for God's sake.

"It's the rules, ma'am." Ed leans back in his chair and motions us forward.

We walk through the entryway and into a lab that's eerily quiet. I punch back my anger and look around. I need to get the lay of the land. The lab jogs my memory. "What did you mean when you said not at the moment?"

"Hmm?"

"I asked if there are more of you and you said not at the moment."

"Jacob, Noah, and Sophia didn't survive the surgeries." Amy wraps a strand of hair around her finger as we walk.

"Didn't survive the surgeries?" I stumble. Joel rights me. Again, icy sweat pops on my skin.

"Other species' body parts aren't always compatible." She continues, her voice devoid of emotion, "Patrick, Marshall, and Marta were sold to other countries."

"Sold?" I jerk my head up. My eye begins to twitch.

"We are some of the most sought after people on earth." Joel points to a door ahead of us. Barely aware of what I'm doing, I push it open, my mind reeling.

"But people don't sell people," I protest, then add, "well if you discount black market babies and sex slaves."

He shrugs and puts his hands in his pockets. "They do here. And since I've never been in the outside world I couldn't say. Besides, we're well looked after. We get the best of everything. We're too valuable not to be taken care of."

I stare at him, not believing what I'm hearing. "But to be treated like a favorite puppy instead of having the freedom of a human being." I shake my head trying to make sense of it. I lift my hand and glance at the sleek leather band on my arm. "It's like an underground electric fence for a dog."

"Excuse me?" Joel raises an eyebrow and tilts his head.

"Never mind."

We walk down another antiseptically-clean hallway. I count the security cameras. There appears to be one every six feet. I stow that fact away, in case I need it later.

"What's it like in the outside world?" Amy asks as we shove through another set of doors.

I shake off my swirling emotions and pay attention to Amy. "For one thing, you have to pay for your own lattes," I say lightly. I look down at my shorts. "And you have more clothes options." Unless you're a dolph-girl trying to maintain a low profile. "To sum it up, it's frustrating, heartbreaking, and wonderful."

"Who'd want frustrating and heartbreaking? Although, the clothes options sound interesting." Her ponytail bounces around her shoulders, except for the escaped wisps she plays with.

"No one wants frustration or heartbreak, but it's part of a package deal. We all want the freedom to make our own decisions whether they're right or wrong. Wouldn't you like to be in the outside world?"

Instead of answering she points. "They would."

We go through another set of double doors. On the other side is a huge tank. My heart lifts then crashes. Three dolphins swim back and forth.

Chapter 29

I run to the tank and place my palm against the glass. My pulse races, beating hard and fast against my wrist. The dolphins circle listlessly. They swim up to the glass to look at my hand. One's tail starts to twitch and it chatters.

"She recognizes you." Amy's eyes widen.

I study her. She's smaller than the rest, younger. Is she one of my rescues?

"Can we swim with them?"

Joel points to a side door. "Suits are in there."

"Let's go in." My heart is beating so hard, I swear it will tear through my ribs. I've got to interact with the dolphins, even if it's just swimming in a tank. To be in the water again with my friends is a form of freedom.

"Sure, why not."

In the next room is a row of swimsuits and trunks, organized by size. I grab a one piece and head for a changing room. I hear the rustle of clothes and shuffle of feet as Amy and Joel follow.

I change quickly and head out. Amy and Joel are waiting. Amy looks cute in a yellow two-piece. Joel looks hot in Hawaiian-style turquoise trunks.

He points to a set of stairs. We take them and climb to the top of the tank and slide into the pool. *Heaven.*

Still chattering, the small dolphin swims to me. She pushes her snout against me. I pet her slick rubbery side.

This is one of my dolphin friends. She must have been captured in my waters, under my watch. Indignation almost chokes me. Fighting it back, I blow bubbles and croon, which comes out chatter similar to hers, "It's all right. It's all right."

We swim together for nearly an hour. Joel and Amy play in the water, doing somersaults and chasing each other and me. The other dolphins begin to play with us. By now the drug I was given has completely worn off. I move with ease.

Joel's play is flirtatious. He tugs gently at my legs and pulls me down deeper. When he slides his arms around me and starts to draw me to him, my little dolphin swims between us, her head pushing us apart. I laugh in delight. Joel grins and mouths, "Foiled."

Amy slips on the back of one and rides it around. The dolphins' lethargy vanishes with playmates.

At one point, the dolphin and I go to the surface to chuff water. Amy and Joel watch fascinated. Without the blowhole, they have to surface more frequently, but still they seem able to stay underwater nearly fifteen minutes without requiring oxygen.

Finally, Joel points to his wrist then the top of the tank. I nod reluctantly and pet the dolphin one last time. I kick upward.

"I'll be back," I bubble to her before I throw my arms around the lip of the pool and pull myself up.

Joel and Amy do the same. Water streams off their sleek bodies. Fluffy white towels lie along the rim of the pool. We are being monitored. I loathe it. "Just like a reality show."

"What?" Joel shakes his head and water flies.

Amy giggles and wipes droplets from her face.

I point to the towels. "Are we being filmed?"

Amy looks confused. Joel makes the connection. "Yeah."

"Lab rats," I mutter.

He gives me a long stare. I see warning in his eyes.

"What did you call us?" Amy stops toweling.

I smile and shoot for reassuring. "Just making a dumb joke. It's not even funny." Not funny at all.

"I've worked up an appetite. Let's get some pizza." Joel tosses his towel on the ground and walks into the changing area.

"Joel's always hungry. But pizza does sound good." Amy pats the towel against the back of her neck.

"Sounds good to me too." I feel like Alice in Wonderland falling down the rabbit hole. We're acting like normal teenagers, when we are so not normal and in the most abnormal situation possible. Maybe it's what keeps Amy and Joel sane.

We follow Joel into the changing station. I glance at the doors, trying to remember which one I'd used to change. They each have a different colored circle at the top. I suppose to help you remember which room you used.

There are a total of ten rooms. Whoever runs this establishment either plans to add more lab rats or has had more in the past. I wonder idly if Dr. Stranger is in charge.

Green. I used the dressing room with the green bulls-eye. I open the door. Yup, there're my clothes. This time I take a moment to look around. There's an aqua indoor-outdoor carpet on the floor with dolphins woven into it. A full-length mirror is hung on one wall. A shelf next to it holds an assortment of combs, hair ties, lotions, and deodorant.

"Just like staying at a five star hotel." My hands on my hips, I look around, checking for a camera. If there is one, I don't see it. I step out of the bathing suit and reach for the crisp shorts. "This is so not me."

I shrug and shimmy into them. I run a brush through my hair, reach to grab the wet strands, draw them back, and put them in a scrunchie before I remember I no longer have to do that. It doesn't matter if people here see me as I am.

Amy and Joel are waiting for me. Amy smiles shyly. I believe she's glad there's another girl around.

Joel holds out his hand. I take it. We walk to the stairs and head down. My dolphin friend follows me on her side of the tank. My heart turns over. My eyes fill. I hastily dash a hand across them. When I get to the bottom, I place my hand against the thick plate of glass. She noses it. "If there's a way, I'll get you back to the sea," I whisper.

"Where does the dolphin recognize you from?" Joel takes my hand again.

"I swam in the ocean near my home. I've either played with her or rescued her at some point in time."

"You swam in the ocean?" Amy's eyes are big.

"Every day." My heart swells.

"Wow."

We walk through the doors and back to the security station. Ed nods and we take the elevator up.

Back in the suite, Joel presses a wall intercom and orders a large pizza with everything. He walks to the stainless steel fridge in the utility alcove. The cherry wood cabinets have a black and brown-splotched granite countertop. Curious, I open a door. My stomach growls in response to the contents: chips, nuts, cookies, candy bars, granola bars, you name it. It's a junk food mecca.

Amy pulls sodas out of the fridge. "Coke?"

"Yeah."

We head for the lounge and the big screen TV that's more the size of a movie screen. There's a portable table with movie seats.

Joel pops in a movie that's only recently hit the theatres. I stare in amazement. What is this place?

"Cool, huh?"

I want to shake him for his complacency. "Don't you want to get out of here?"

For a brief moment, anger burns high and hot in his eyes. I take a quick step back. The look disappears as quickly as it came, replaced by his habitual indolent attitude. "And what do you suggest we do about the trackers, cut them out of our arms? I was told that process could be particularly unpleasant. They were fitted to attach to a nerve."

A shudder glides down my spine like a spider. "I'm sorry," I whisper. He shrugs.

The elevator dings. An attendant steps off balancing a large pizza. She places it on the table along with disposable plates and napkins, then goes to the alcove. She also wears a Taser. Joel and Amy dig in. I've lost my appetite.

Under cover of the movie, Joel leans toward me. "What you said about the outside world, frustration and heartache, would you go back to it if you could?"

"I will at the first opportunity," I whisper fiercely. My thoughts turn to Gramps. Has my disappearance put too much stress on his weak heart? And what about Tyler? Is he frantic with worry or thinking good riddance?

I look around me at my velvet-lined prison and rub my fingers down my face.

"Do you have family waiting for you?"

I nod again. Thinking of home is almost more than I can bear. I move my fingers to my arms and dig into the fleshy portion to keep from breaking down. If I start to cry, I'll never stop.

"Amy and I will be your family." His lips touch mine. His breath is salty and cool from the pizza and Coke he's just sipped.

His touch and words comfort me. But worry about Gramps is like the sea's undercurrent. It may be hidden beneath the surface but it's always there.

"Thank you." I don't wish to burden him further with my concerns.

We settle in to watch the movie. He's on one side and Amy on my other. We've completely polished off the pizza, due in large part to Joel. He holds my hand. The feel of his fingers wrapped around mine is seductive. For this small moment in time, my worries recede.

We fix popcorn and watch more movies. By midnight, Amy is yawning. I rise. "I'm ready to call it a day."

"I'll see you tomorrow, Piper." Amy stretches and heads for her room. I notice it's on the other side of the lounge from mine.

I turn to Joel. "Where's your room?"

He smiles and leans in. "If you're interested, I'd be happy to show you." The dolphin in me kicks to the surface, interested. My human side remembers the monitors…and Tyler.

"That's a fascinating offer, but not tonight."

"Then, I'll hope for tomorrow." He smiles easily. "I'll see you to your room."

"That's not necessary."

"No, it's not."

He takes my hand and leads me to my door. "If you change your mind, I'm on the other side of the lounge, west wing."

I lift my head to nod and his lips claim mine. It's a soft lazy kiss, sexy like Joel himself. My lips part. His tongue does a slow exploration of my mouth. With the finesse of a dancer, he withdraws.

I stare at him, my lids heavy, my mind swirling.

His hands on my shoulders, he kisses me lightly on the forehead. "Good night, Piper."

"Good night." I manage to get out.

He walks away, hands in pockets, whistling. For a moment, he turns. "West wing. You're welcome anytime." He winks and saunters off.

"Surreal." My mind is still whirling as I step into my room. I notice aqua cotton boxers and an aqua cotton cami have been laid on my bed. "Must be the fricking fairy godmaid." I shuck my clothes and fall into bed.

"Well, Gramps, my worst fears have been realized. I'm a lab rat. The surroundings aren't exactly what I expected but it doesn't change the fact I'm here for experimentation," I whisper in the dark. Finally, the tears I can no longer keep at bay fall. I cry till I think I can't possibly cry anymore. My tears ducts must be dried out by now, but salty wet liquid continues to pour down my cheeks. I bury my face in the pillow to muffle my sobs and cry some more.

Exhausted, I finally fall asleep only to toss and turn. Half-formed dreams try to surface. Gramps sitting in a wheelchair, on the beach, his arms outstretched. Tyler running through the sand, his feet sinking into the tiny granules, frantically calling my name. A pod of dolphins swimming back and forth along the shoreline searching for me. I run toward them but they don't see me. I call but they don't hear. Once again, tears stream down my face. I stumble and fall, scraping my arm on a broken shell. I jerk it away.

"There, there, it's just a bad dream." The needle clatters to the floor. Casey bends over to pick it up. I wonder if she managed to get drugs in me. By the mess on the floor, I'd say not.

"Tsk. Tsk." She clicks her tongue as she cleans up the mess. "I'll have to get another syringe."

"Please, no more shots. They make me feel..." I search for the word. "Heavy," I finally say inadequately.

"I'll check with the doctor and let you know. He wants to see you in forty-five minutes. You've got time to take a quick shower. I'll bring you a cup of coffee."

"Thank you," I mumble, still shaken by the dreams. I do not want to see Dr. Stranger. Thinking of him breaks me out in a cold sweat. Something bad is going to happen. I know it.

My hear pounds and my breath quickens. I stumble into the bathroom and turn on the shower. Along with the water comes a fine mist scented of vanilla and heather. I step into the soothing waters and let them pour over me. I lift my face hoping the water will offset the red blotches on my face from my crying jag.

I look toward the mirror. My eyes are puffy and red. Considering the abuse they got last night, I'm lucky to be able to open them. After toweling off and blow drying my hair, I walk into my bedroom to find a silk tee and navy shorts laid out, along with navy sandals. I sigh. I feel like a Barbie-doll. Having my clothes chosen for me is almost as bad as my nerd attire back home.

I look around. True to her word, Casey has left a cup of coffee in a to-go cup on the table. The strong arabica aroma tickles my nostrils. I inhale then sip. *Ah.* I wait for the kick of caffeine and after a moment realize there isn't going to be one. They've given me decaf. Do they think decaf will keep me calm for the upcoming meeting? Right.

A knock sounds at the door. Casey sticks her head in. "Are you ready?"

"Yeah." I get up and follow her out. The thick carpet masks the thump of our shoes. The rustle of her crisp white uniform is the only sound in the hall. It seems an out-of-date touch for such a young woman.

We ride the elevator to the second floor and proceed to Dr. Stranger's office. With each step it gets harder to breathe. By the time she knocks on the door, I'm clasping my throat, on the verge of a full-blown panic attack.

She frowns. "Are you all right?"

I give a faint nod. "I'm all right," I manage to get out and hope I will be in an hour.

"Enter." The voice is emotionless.

We walk in. He motions to a chair in front of the desk. "Sit."

I sit.

"I'll call you when I'm done." He dismisses Casey with a wave of his hand.

"Yes, sir."

I half expect her to curtsey. The thick door swings silently shut behind her.

He studies me. "How has your stay been so far?"

I stare straight ahead, my hands clasped tightly together.

He ignores my silence. "I have plans for you, Piper."

I look at him, then look away.

"Plans that will make you one of the most important women in the world."

I want to scream. I have no desire to be one of the most important women in the world. I'm fine with my current nonentity status. I think of all those times I bitched and moaned about hiding behind a nerd identity. It doesn't look nearly so bad now. Gramps was right, things can always be worse.

Dr. Stranger continues, "I don't want you to think you'd be forced into anything distasteful or plebian. The project will be handled scientifically."

I wipe my clammy hands on my shorts. I've got a feeling plebian would be better.

"Do you know what IVF is?"

For the first time I respond, "In vitro fertilization."

"Very good." He rubs his hands together and smiles at me like I'm his prized student. At least, I assume the grimace is his attempt at a smile. "That's correct. In vitro fertilization. Sperm and egg are combined in a laboratory dish. Next the embryo is transferred to the uterus."

"IVF makes it much easier to add dolphin DNA." He leans back in the chair looking pleased with himself. "Do you realize how lucky you are?"

Oh, yeah, teenagers are standing in line to be lab rats.

"Like Eve, you are one of a kind. Only your child will be my creation. I'll be its God." Shocked, I notice the fanatical gleam in his eyes and quickly look away.

"Your child will be the most sought-after child in the universe."

My child. A lab rat. Sold to the highest bidder. Terror grips me. Fear for a child that hasn't been conceived fills me.

"When was your last period?"

"Excuse me?" My head jerks up.

"I'm a doctor, Piper, your doctor."

Do I tell the truth? Do I lie?

"Come, come, my dear. That sort of thing is only too easy to track."

I cave. "Two weeks."

"Two weeks? Perfect." He actually beams.

My stomach muscles tighten. "Why?"

"The time would be perfect. Let's get some blood samples and do an ultrasound."

"No." I jump to my feet.

"Not to worry, my dear, you won't feel a thing."

He presses the intercom on his desk. "Casey, bring a mild sedative for Piper."

"Yes, doctor." Her voice is tinny.

"I don't want a sedative." I fight back panic.

"It will lower your stress level."

"I don't want it." My breathing is shallow, my heart is racing. I jump to my feet. Before I can say more, Casey comes bustling in with a syringe.

"Just relax, Piper." He steps around the desk, places a hand on my shoulder. I knock it off and make a dash for the door.

Casey comes at me with the syringe. Dr. Stranger grabs me from behind and locks his arms around me. I thrash wildly. "Stay away from me," I yell as Casey plunges the syringe deep into my skin. "Stay away." My voice is slow and disjointed.

The response to the drug is immediate. I calm. But deep beneath the calm is terror.

"Take a blood sample, check her vitals, and get her prepped for an ovarian ultrasound."

"Of course, doctor."

The words come from a long way off.

Casey leads me through an adjoining door into a chamber with an examining table and a changing room. She points toward the changing room. "Take off your clothes and put on the gown. It opens in the front."

She shuts the door. I slump into the chair.

Casey knocks on the door. "Ready?"

I don't respond

Sandra Cox

She opens it and undresses me before leading me to the examining table. "Just lay down, Piper."

"I don't want to."

She nudges me down.

Dr. Stranger walks in and snaps on gloves. "Put your feet in the stirrups. Now just relax, Piper."

I close my eyes and ignore him. My legs are lifted into the stirrups. Moments later, I feel a probe against my vaginal wall. It doesn't hurt, but it's weird.

"It's there." His voice is filled with excitement. I force open my heavy lids and see him point to a screen over my head.

"Give her a mild injection and we'll harvest it."

Injection? Harvest? "No." I protest then feel a tiny prick in my arm. I go deeper into my dream state, in and out of consciousness. I see what looks like a long, fine needle in his hand, then nothing.

In a dream, I think I hear him say, "I have it. Give me the Petri dish."

* * * *

I wake up in my room. Casey is sitting in a chair next to me, reading a fashion magazine. I push up on my elbows. I feel groggy and my insides are sore.

Casey gets up and smiles. "How are you, sleepyhead?"

"What happened? What did you do to me?"

She takes my vitals. "Nothing, silly. You had a little exam."

Little exam?

"The doctor wants you to take plenty of fluids and protein. What would you like?"

I'm starved. "Coke. Hamburger and fries."

"You've got it. Here take a sip of this and I'll go get your food." She holds my head up. I sip water from a straw. She lays my head back down and I close my eyes.

The next thing I know, my bed is being raised—I didn't even know it had that capability—and a tray placed on my lap. The aroma is wonderful. I am so hungry.

I take a bite of the juicy burger and immediately feel better. Casey pops the top of a Coke and the dark liquid fizzes over ice. She hands it to me. I drink thirstily.

"The doctor wants you to rest today. Tomorrow it's back to normal."

"Whatever normal may be."

She giggles gaily.

"What happened to me yesterday?"

"Nothing. You had a yearly, that's all. When you're finished, just set the tray outside the door. I'll pick it up later."

After she leaves, I polish off my burger and fries. Whatever medication they've given me—again—is wearing off. I want to see my dolphin. I need to see her. We share a link. We're both captives in this awful place.

I get up, get dressed, and head for the first floor where I flash my wristband at Ed and walk through the hall, and several doorways, to the tank.

By the time, I get there, I'm fairly winded. I can't understand why I'm so tired. What did they do to me?

I look in the tank. Two dolphins swim listlessly back and forth paying me little attention.

My dolphin is gone.

Chapter 30

I stumble to Dr. Stranger's office. Without waiting for an invitation, I throw open the door. On the verge of hysteria, I demand, "Where's my dolphin?"

Dr. Stranger raises a thin gray eyebrow. He stares at me from behind his glasses. "What are you doing out of bed?"

"Where's my dolphin?"

"Your dolphin?" The eyebrow goes higher.

"Yes, mine. We visited them yesterday. There were three, now there are only two."

He takes off his glasses, whips out a handkerchief, wipes the lenses, and then puts them back on. "The third dolphin is fine. We needed her for an experiment we're working on. She'll be back in the tank tomorrow."

Memory of his voice, triumphant but murky, saying "We've harvested the egg," makes my heart beat wildly and my breath whoosh in and out way to fast. Or did I dream it? I have no tolerance for meds. They do weird things to me. It has to be a dream. I refuse to consider anything else. "Does her experiment have anything to do with me?"

He rises and puts his hand on my shoulder. My skin crawls. This man may have killed my mother. "Of course not," he says soothingly. "Now go back to your room and rest. Everything is fine."

My breathing shallow, I head back to my room. I'm exhausted. I'll just lie down for a moment.

A knock on the door wakes me. The room is dim and shadowed. I must have slept for several hours. Rubbing my eyes, I stumble to the door and open it.

"Hey, where have you been all day?" Joel leans his lanky form against the door frame, his arms crossed.

"Tests."

"Gotcha." He nods. "Want to grab something to eat?"

"Sure. Where's Amy?"

"Reading a book. Are you ready? We can eat in the alcove."

"Okay. Do you mind if we check on the dolphins first?"

He gives me a puzzled look but agrees. "No problem."

I'm sore and walk slower than normal. My stomach is achy.

"Hey, are you okay?" He throws a companionable arm around my shoulder.

"Yeah, I'm okay."

"Those tests can be a bitch."

"Tell me about it." I raise my eyebrows and heave out a breath.

"Those tests can…"

"Never mind," I interrupt hastily.

He grins.

"Ha. Ha."

I don't run but I pick up my pace when I near the tank. "She's back!"

"Who's back?"

I point. "My dolphin was missing. He used her for experiments." I step closer to the tank. She approaches. "She doesn't look that great, does she?" Her eyes have a film on them, her skin looks dull and there is some type of waterproof bandage on her head.

Joel squints and studies her. "She looked better yesterday."

"How do they get them in and out of the tank?"

He opens a closet door, placed discreetly in a recess near the tank, points to buttons on the wall that are similar to elevator buttons.

I look at him and raise my brows.

"The button on the right lifts up a partition that divides this tank and a smaller one. The button on the left leads back to the ocean."

Excitement courses through me. "Have you ever tried to free them?"

He stares into the tank, his face expressionless. "Once, a long time ago."

"What happened?"

"She swam back to me. The next experiment, she didn't survive."

"Oh, Joel, I'm sorry." Horror replaces enthusiasm.

He shrugs. "Like I said, it was a long time ago."

I turn to the tank and stare at my dolphin. "What happens if I free her?"

"An alarm will go off. Ed is probably watching you right now."

I turn back to the tank. "Is he the only guard here?"

"Technically, he's the only guard on the first floor. There are several attendants floating around. Plus there's guards stationed outside. The alarm would alert them."

Sandra Cox

My head hurts. I rub it. "I wish I weren't so tired. I can't think. I don't know what to do."

"Why not sleep on it? She'll be here tomorrow."

I think I hear him mutter, "I hope."

I put my hand on the glass. She nuzzles it. "I'll find a way to get you home. I promise." Watching her hurts my heart.

She chatters.

I remove my hand and we walk away. Before we go through the first set of doors, I look back. My handprint is on the glass and the dolphin is still beside it.

Exhaustion overcomes me. I stagger. Joel puts his arm around my waist. I lean against him. "You've had quite a day haven't you?"

"Yeah, I guess."

The walls blur. My legs feel like water and my knees start to give. His grip tightens. "Hold on. I'll get you to your room."

I nod. My head falls to his shoulder.

"Did you leave a boyfriend behind?" He pushes through the swinging double doors.

"Yes. No. It's complicated."

"I think I'll take the no. I like that answer best."

Joel raises his hand as we pass the security station then slip onto the elevator.

I look at the buttons, one through four. Joel presses four.

I've been on every floor but three. "What's on the third floor?"

"Labs." Joel's voice sounds strained.

I shake my head feeling muzzy. "But the labs are on the first floor."

"Those are general labs. Blood work, that sort of thing."

I'm confused. Normally, I can pick up on whatever it is he's not saying, but I'm not at my best right now. "What's on third?"

"The experimental labs."

"Oh." My voice trails off. I wish I hadn't asked. I close my eyes. Experimental labs are the last thing I want to think of right now.

I'm barely awake when we get to my door. As if I'm no more than a feather, he picks me up and lays me on the bed. "Sweet dreams, Piper." He kisses my forehead and leaves.

"Good night." I fall into an exhausted sleep.

* * * *

"Good morning, Piper." Casey's perky voice wakes me. I don't know how long I slept but it had to be a good ten hours. Other than being ravenous, I feel better.

"Good morning."

"Dr. Stranger would like to see you."

"Again?"

"Yes. More blood work."

"I'm hungry."

"Shower and I'll order your breakfast. What would you like?"

"Coffee and a bowl of oatmeal."

"It'll be here when you get through. I'll be back in forty-five minutes."
She gives me her usual cheery smile and leaves.

I shower, blow-dry my hair, and put on the shorts and top that is laid
out. This time the shorts are blue and pink plaid with a pink top.

The oatmeal and coffee are sitting on the table in front of the couch.
Memories of Gramps, and the many times he's fixed me this breakfast,
crash down on me. My throat tightens. I will not cry. I repeat it like a
mantra until I can take a breath and look at my meal with equanimity.

I plop on the couch, take my first sip of coffee. My world rights. It
may be decaf but it has a wonderful flavor. If I order coffee when I'm not
seeing Stranger, would they send me caffeinated? Cranberries and pecans
sit in a separate dish to sprinkle on the oatmeal. I take a deep breath and
dig in.

With uncanny timing, Casey comes back as I finish the last mouthful.
She keeps up a running dialogue as we walk down the hall.

Dr. Stranger glances up from his computer as I enter. His office is a lot
like him, well appointed but cold and sterile.

"That will be all, Casey."

"Yes, sir."

"How are you feeling, Piper?" He motions toward the black leather
chair in front of the desk.

I sit on the edge of the chair, my spine straight. "I'm fine."

He looks at me over his glasses. "We're going to start hormone
injections today."

"Excuse me?"

"We are going to start hormone injections."

"Why?"

"To help you produce more eggs."

"My eggs are fine the way they are." Embarrassed heat floods my face.
I wouldn't want to have this conversation with my own doctor, let alone
this madman.

"For a normal girl, yes. But you are so much more. You are an amazing
creation. A creation we would like to duplicate."

"What you are doing can't be legal." If I can keep him talking, maybe I can find something out and when I do, I'll blow his operation sky high.

He flicks his hand as if to wave off such a trivial notion. "Science is above legalities and so are you."

I can't decide whether to run screaming from the room or dive for his throat. The throat.

As if he read my mind, he says, "If you don't cooperate, I could always use Amy. She's a sweet little thing, don't you think?"

Appalled, I whisper, "She's only fifteen."

"Yes, but she's a mature fifteen. And if that doesn't bring you around there's always 'your'"—he makes quotation marks with his fingers—"dolphin."

"You bastard." I jump from my seat and spring toward him.

"Don't think I won't do it."

I let my hands drop to my side. I was so close to having them around his scrawny throat I could feel his body heat. My chest heaves. I force out the words, loathing it. "You win. Did you try to harvest eggs from me yesterday?"

He leans back in his chair and smiles tolerantly. "Why do you ask that?"

"Because I remember you saying something about getting or finding one."

"You don't need to worry about your eggs until it's time to fertilize and implant them."

Oh my God. My breath stutters in my throat. I dig down deep. Gramps didn't raise a quitter is my mantra. I bring it out and repeat it whenever I need to give myself strength. Somehow I'll be out of here by then. And I'll free the dolphins and take Amy and Joel with me, even if I have to cut their trackers out myself.

"Let's go into the examining room."

"Why?"

"I'm going to give you an injection on the fatty portion of your stomach."

"I don't have any fat on my stomach." I want to hide my head. What a stupid thing to say. It just slipped out. I must be more nervous than I thought, but maybe that's the way to play it. Let him think he's won. That's he's just dealing with a typical teenager worried about her looks.

He laughs. "Don't worry, it won't hurt."

"I don't have any belly fat," I mutter.

"Hop up on the table."

He draws fluid into a syringe. His thumb on the plunger, he pushes down to release air. Liquid spurts like a miniature fountain. "Lift up your shirt please and unzip your shorts."

I look at the door and give serious consideration to making a break for it.

He looks at me and guesses my thoughts. "I'd rather not strap you down, but I will without hesitation if you don't do exactly as I say. Remember Amy and your dolphin."

I look in his eyes and know he means it. I bite my lip and comply.

After I do, he swabs my tummy and presses the needle into my skin. Moments later, he's done. "There, that wasn't bad was it?"

I don't answer.

"Tomorrow, we'll get a tracker chip in you."

As if I'm his damn pet. I bite my lips together. I will not scream. I will not scream.

"I'll call Casey to come and get you."

"I can find my way back." I scoot off the table.

"Good, I'm glad you are feeling comfortable here. It's your home now. We like our subjects to be happy."

As if this hellish place could ever be my home. My lips curl. "Why?"

"That's a good question. It's easier for everyone, myself included. When I first started my work, I didn't realize how important it was to keep the subjects happy." He shrugged. "Trial and error."

Without responding, I walk through the door. Once on the other side, my breath goes out in a whoosh. I hate that man. He's creepy, a modern day Dr. Frankenstein. I wonder if he tried to keep my mother content or if she was one of the trial and errors in the happy department.

Determined to put distance between myself and Dr. Stranger, I go in search of Joel and Amy.

I spend the rest of the day with my new friends. We make a couple of trips to the tank to check on the dolphins, mine in particular. I know she pines for the sea and her own pod. We swim with them for about forty minutes. That seems to cheer her up, though her color still isn't good.

From there, we spend the evening playing games on the Xbox in the lounge pretending we're normal teenagers, not mutant lab rats. I've never had time for video games. I decide I like them. They keep the dark at bay.

Curious, I ask Joel and Amy what they do about schooling. They tell me most of their courses are online. For a moment, I think about Rosemont. I'm a bit nostalgic. I wouldn't even mind seeing Edgar the Asshole. My situation has to be bad if Fahrenbacher looks good.

At eleven, I'm ready to go to my room. They're beating my socks off anyway. My attention is elsewhere. It has been all day, trying to figure out how to get us out of here. Deep into the game, Joel doesn't offer to walk me to my room, just waves absently.

The game den is at the farthest end of the lounge. I walk past the alcove where the snacks are stored, and head to my room.

Once there, I change into thin sweats, randomly grab a book from the shelf and turn on the TV. Anything to take my mind off today's events. It's unusual to do absolutely nothing productive. Tomorrow I'll talk to Joel, feel him out. Underneath that casual, boyish charm, I sense deep passion. He just keeps it buried so no one can see it. For now, my brain is cooked. I need to recharge, escape this place mentally if not physically.

I can't get into the book. I toss it on the bed and surf the TV. The door opens. Amy and Joel must have finished their game and decided to come in for a while.

My breath catches. It's not Amy or Joel. Shoulders hunched forward, I clutch the blanket in an age-old gesture of protection. "Who are you?"

A dark-haired man in a black diving suit slips in. He's lean and muscled, and his eyes spell danger. He puts his finger to his lips. Someone else slides in behind him.

My breath catches in my throat. Tears well up and spill over. "Tyler! How did you find me? You came for me."

Again the diver motions me to silence.

"Your distress watch," Tyler whispers. In three long strides, he crosses the room and scoops me into his arms. "Are you all right?" His arms are tight around me, his heart thumps rapid and hard.

"Oh my God, you're here." I touch his face, unable to believe it, afraid I'm asleep and dreaming.

"Are you all right?" he repeats urgently, clasping my arms.

"I am now." Relief floods me. I push my head into his shoulder. We stand there silent, holding each other.

The stranger in the wetsuit comes closer. "We've got to get you out of here."

"Where are we going?" I mumble into Tyler's shoulder.

"My uncle and I have come to take you home."

I raise my head and study the man with interest. "Oh, you must be his uncle in the Mafia."

"For God sakes, Piper." Tyler exclaims in low tones.

"Mafia?" his uncle whispers.

"This is my Uncle Jackson Sweet. The SEAL I told you about."

"Oh, yeah, sorry." Once again, my mouth has worked before my brain. Before the conversation can go further downhill, the door opens again. In one smooth motion, Jackson grabs Tyler and steps behind the door.

"Hey, Piper, I was wondering if you wanted some company." Joel steps into the room.

"Finished the game, huh?"

"Yeah, trounced her. So do you want company?" He moves forward. There's a gleam in his eyes. His lips tilt up and he reaches out his arms.

I chew on the tip of my index finger and glance over his shoulder. "Actually, I've got company, Joel."

Tyler and Jackson step forward. I notice Tyler's teeth are clenched.

The boys size each other up.

Joel's sharp gaze takes them both in. He drawls, "This wouldn't be the boyfriend that's not really a boyfriend, would it?"

"What the hell is that supposed to mean?" Tyler snaps and moves toward Joel.

"What are you doing here?" Joel growls.

"We've come to take her home."

Joel pauses. His whole demeanor changes. After a long uneasy moment, he nods. "It would be in her best interest. She doesn't belong here."

The tension in the room notches down, Tyler visibly relaxes.

Before he can answer, the door swings open, again. Tyler and his uncle dive behind it. An attendant dressed in white, carrying a metal basket filled with empty vials and a syringe, stands in the doorway. The light from the hall halos her. She's young, blonde and pretty, a few years older than Joel, perhaps. He lounges against the open door, giving the two men cover and a chance to slide into the bathroom. "What are you doing here, sweet cheeks?"

"I could ask you the same thing," she responds tartly.

Uh-oh. There may not be any dolph-girls around, but it looks like Joel's made at least one human conquest.

"I asked first." He gives her a lazy, teasing smile.

"I came to take blood."

He arches a brow. "Isn't it a bit late for that?"

"Dr. Stranger's orders."

He sweeps out a hand. "Be my guest. I'm just leaving."

The pretty girl stalks over to me. I raise my arm. She jabs in the needle hard enough to make me jump. She fills several vials with blood and leaves, never speaking to me.

"You can come out," I say softly.

Jackson and Tyler glide cautiously out of the bathroom.

"We better get moving," Jackson says.

There's a soft knock on the door. Joel slides inside.

"Are there any guards on this floor?" Jackson asks Joel.

"No, but there's hall cameras. Oh and one attendant, but he wasn't around when I came in."

"We took care of the cameras. Or I should say my nephew did." He gives a quick grin and thumbs up to Tyler. "He's a whiz with electronics."

"He must be," Joel says.

"I didn't know that," I admit.

Jackson cracks the door and looks out. "Let's go."

Impulsively, I reach for Joel's arm. "Come with us."

His face softens. For a moment, his hand covers mine. "I can't leave Amy."

"Of course not, bring her."

"Piper, I'm wearing a tracker."

Jackson shuts the door. "What do you mean? Take it off, man, and let's go."

"Unfortunately, it's buried under the skin and before you suggest cutting it out, I was told they've taken pains to make sure it stays in place."

Jackson whirls in my direction. "Do you have one, too?"

I lift up my wrist and show the band. "I was to be fitted tomorrow."

"What is this place?" He demands as he whips a deadly-looking knife from his scabbard and cuts the band from my arm. It falls harmlessly to the floor.

"Not now, Uncle J." Tyler shifts from one foot to another. He, too, is dressed in a black diver suit. He rubs his knuckles with his fingertips, his expression edgy.

"You better go." Joel nods and gives me a small smile that doesn't reach his eyes.

"I don't want to leave you here."

He places a finger over my lips. I feel more than see Tyler and Jackson exchange glances.

"When I figure out how to get rid of this tracker, I'll find you. I promise."

"I'm in Santa Cruz County, in a little town call Ortega."

Tyler cuts in. "We've got to go before somebody finds the guards we knocked out."

I remember my dolphin. I can't believe I've forgotten her, even for a minute. "There's something I've got to do first."

"I'll do it." Joel looks at me. He knows exactly what I'm thinking.
"Are you sure?"

He turns toward Tyler. "The security screens and alarms are down, right?"

Tyler gives a short jerk of his chin.

"Leave it to me. Now go."

"Thank you." I walk over and kiss his cheek.

He turns into me and kisses me swift and hard. "Go."

"Take good care of her," he tells Tyler.

"Kiss her again, and I'll break your face."

"You're welcome to try."

They eye each other like snarling dogs. The strain in the room thickens.

"We don't have time for this," Jackson snaps, exasperated.

His cheeks flushed, a pinched expression on his face, Tyler leads me to the door, his hand possessively on my arm. Jackson steps in front of us, takes a quick look around, and motions us through.

"Wait a minute. I'll be right back." Joel steps out.

Tyler and Jackson look at each other. Jackson looks at his watch. "He's got two minutes; then we're out of here." He concentrates on his watch.

Tyler shifts from one foot to the other. He throws me a worried glance before looking quickly away.

"All right let's go." Jackson reaches for the door as Joel comes through it. He's holding two lab coats. "They keep them in the closet in case the dietician or a technician spills anything on their coats. You've probably noticed this is a pretty sterile environment."

"Thanks, kid." Jackson and Tyler quickly slip on the coats. They cover enough of the wet suits that they can pass for attendants if they're not looked at too closely. Even their black water shoes will pass inspection. He holds out his hand to Joel. "I'll be back for you. It won't be tonight. After the guards wake up, all hell's going to break loose. But I'll be back."

Joel nods. "I've got to get going. I've got a job of my own to do." He winks at me and saunters out.

We slip out behind him. I start down the dim lit hall toward the elevator. Jackson grabs my arm and heads in the other direction.

"Hey you, where are you going?" An attendant steps out of the elevator. He puts his hand on his Taser.

Jackson turns and walks toward the young man. "Hi there. Tonight's my first night on the job. I don't think we've met. I'm Henry Mason." He holds out his hand.

"Stuart Puckett. Where are you headed with the dolph?" He eyes Jackson suspiciously.

If the question throws Jackson, he gives no sign of it. "Taking her down for blood work."

"At this hour?" The attendant purses his lips.

"I just do what I'm told." Jackson shrugs.

The attendant nods, but is still frowning. "Why the stairs?"

Jackson throws up his hands. "You found me out. I've got a phobia about elevators. Was stuck in one for nine freaking hours once. By the time I got out of there I'd nearly wet my pants. I've never been in one since. You don't think the boss will mind do ya? Want to come with us? You can give me some tips on hooking up with that cute blonde tech that works in the lab."

Stuart's hand falls away from his Taser. "I've got work to do. I'll catch you later. And good luck hooking up with the blonde. She thinks she's better than the rest of us."

Jackson nods. "Yeah, the cute ones know it. Thanks. See you around." Whistling, he guides me through a door I never noticed before.

"That was close," Tyler says in a low voice.

"Yeah, we need to get moving." In the dim recesses, both he and Tyler slip off the lab coats.

As we start down the stairs, our feet give light thuds against the steel steps. At least, mine and Tyler's do. Jackson's make no sound at all. "What was the kid talking about when he said he had a job to do?" he asks, his voice pitched low.

"He's freeing the dolphins."

"Dolphins? What the hell goes on in this place anyway? And why did they refer to you as a dolph?"

Tyler interrupts, "Not now, Uncle J."

Jackson shrugs and picks up the pace. Before we get to the first stairwell, he halts, puts his finger to his lips, and pushes back against the wall. We hide in the shadows. I bite my lips, my palms sweaty. I have to force myself not to shift from foot to foot.

Two female attendants head down the stairs chattering. "I can't believe you're making me walk instead of taking the elevator," one complains. They are so close the scent of perfume wafts over us. I close my eyes, scrunch up my face, and try not to breathe, afraid I'll sneeze.

"I've gained five pounds. I need the stairs." Their chatter gets fainter. A door opens and closes.

We move forward. Minutes later, we're at the bottom of the stairwell. Jackson opens the door a crack and looks around. I smell the scent of trees and sea salt. I'm almost giddy. It seems like forever since I smelled the sea.

Jackson motions us forward. A cool breeze blows, ruffling my hair and caressing my skin. I pull air deep into my lungs.

I hear a muffled sound near my feet. Two men are bound. Both have duct tape around their mouths.

Jackson turns to me and Tyler. "Keep low and run." His voice is a bare whisper of sound. He bends down and starts jogging down a rocky incline.

Small rocks and pebbles go cascading downward as I slip and slide. Nerves have stiffened my limbs. "Be careful," Jackson whispers.

My night vision kicks in and I'm more stable on my feet. Behind me, Tyler steadies me with a hand on my waist.

We continue our plunge downward. The moon travels behind a cloud. Pines rustle. An owl hoots. The sounds of the sea grow stronger.

There's a shout from up above. Floodlights go on. My shoulders tighten.

"Come on, we're almost there." Jackson steps up the pace. We're running flat out now, pebbles and rocks cascade down the rocky slope. Water laps against the shore.

"Can you swim?" he asks me.

Tyler snorts. "Like a fish." He hasn't said much since he broke in to rescue me.

I see the water and run toward it, kicking off my sandals, and disrobing as I enter the shallows. First my top floats away, next my sweats.

When the water hits my waist I dive, cavorting like the dolphin I partially am. I turn somersaults. The water ripples and splashes around me. I feel a touch on my arm. It's Jackson. He points ahead and to my right. A boat is drifting. I nod and head toward it, easily outdistancing them.

The freedom of the water is wonderful, euphoric. I wish I could stay in it forever.

A spotlight hits me, reminding me of the situation and the danger we're still in. Jackson motions that he's going back. I assume to take care of whoever is responsible for the spotlight. I dive under and swim for the boat.

I reach it, climb the rope ladder hanging over the side, and pull myself up. Water runs off me in rivulets. I push my hair out of my eyes.

Arms circle me. "Oh, Piper," Holly sobs.

"Holly?" Emotion washes over me and I hug her hard.

"Piper, are you all right?"

"I am now." My voice is muffled against her shoulder.

She steps back and looks at me. "You're in your underwear. You're beautiful, but I knew beneath the geek attire you would be. And your voice is different than it normally is."

"Just don't come on to me," I tease. She gives a shaky laugh. I turn to the water and watch the shore. The light goes out. Minutes crawl by. Finally, Jackson, followed by Tyler, slithers over the side. Water splashes us as they stand up.

After she's sure her brother and uncle are all right, she turns to me and demands, "What happened? Who kidnapped you and why?"

Before I can reply, Tyler interrupts, "No questions, Hol."

My heart warms. Not only is he not demanding an explanation, he's bending over backward to help me keep my secret.

"Take her downstairs and get her some dry clothes. And remember, Hol. No questions. She's been through enough."

"Come with me." She tugs gently on my arm.

We go below deck. I look around the well-appointed cabin. "Whose cruiser?"

"Not sure. Jackson borrowed it from the dock. I brought some extra clothes for you." She hugs me again. "I'm so glad you're all right. We've been worried sick about you."

She hands me a pair of thin sweats and a T-shirt. I pull them on and giggle. Holly is considerably shorter and bustier than I am. The pants are short and the top loose.

The lulling motion of the boat soothes me. I inhale the tang of salt air and yawn. I sit down on the berth. "If you don't mind, Hol, I think I'll rest for a minute." Emotionally, I'm exhausted. I lie down. The pillow has a musty scent but I don't care.

Holly throws a brown cover over me. It smells of fish. I don't mind that, either. I wonder if Joel has succeeded in freeing the dolphins and if so, what's happened to him.

"Sure." Her voice comes from a long way off. I have no inkling how much time passes but the next thing I'm aware of is being lifted in hard arms and held against cool, smooth material that's slightly damp.

"I'll get the SUV." The voice sounds like Jackson's. I'm too tired to open my eyes. I drift back to sleep.

I must be dreaming because I hear Gramps say, "You found her." His voice is shaky. "I owe you. Anything you want."

In the dream someone says, "You can't give me what I want."

I roll over. I feel the feather light touch of lips on my forehead before once again I'm asleep.

Chapter 31

The rough cry of a seagull wakes me. Interesting, I don't remember hearing gulls at the clinic. I stretch. My heel finds a tiny crevice. I frown. My bed at the clinic has a perfect mattress whereas my mattress at home…

I sit straight up and look around. "I'm home!" The smells of pancakes, warm syrup, and coffee draw me. "Gramps!" I scream and race for the kitchen.

Holding a spatula, a white apron wrapped around his middle, he turns and holds out his arms. Tears are in his eyes. "My girl." I bury my head in his thin chest. I don't remember Gramps being this skinny. The scent of Old Spice blends with the kitchen aromas.

"I was afraid I'd never see you again." His voice is husky. His arms tremble. "What happened? Where were you?"

Just thinking of where I was has my muscles tightening. I draw back and rub my head. A headache is brewing. "At the experimental labs. If you don't mind, I don't want to talk about it right now." I rub my clammy hands on my sweats.

"All right. Sit. Sit. I fixed you pancakes. Let me pour you coffee."

"I'll get the coffee." I reach into the cabinet, pull out two thick white mugs, and fill them full of the dark steaming brew. The aromatic moisture rises from the coffee and tickles my nostrils.

"I don't think you're supposed to have pancakes."

He heaves a sigh. "I'm having oatmeal."

"Let me help."

"Get out the syrup then."

I dig in the fridge and pull out the syrup. Gramps sets a stack of golden brown pancakes with butter melting in the center in front of me.

"Eat it while it's hot. I'll get my oatmeal."

I take a mouthful and sigh with bliss. I'm home.

He tosses his apron on the counter, scoops up his oatmeal, adds milk, and sits down. I lay down my fork and look at him. "I'm sorry I added to your stress. Are you okay?"

"I'm fine, and it's not your fault, dear girl. I don't want to push you, but can you tell me anything? Are you in danger? Do I need to get you out of here?"

"I don't know." Suddenly, it all comes tumbling out. I tell him about Joel, Amy and my dolphins. And the ghastly doctor.

"What day is it?" I ask around a mouthful of pancakes.

"Tuesday."

"I better get to school. What did you tell them?"

"That you had a virus."

"Good idea." I nod.

He stirs his oatmeal. It dribbles from his spoon as he lifts it. "Tyler's idea. He promised me he'd get you back and he did. He's a good young man, Piper. Trustworthy."

I swallow a lump in my throat. "I know, Gramps. The best."

"Why don't you stay home today? Get your sea-legs back."

"Now that's an offer I don't hear every day," I joke, then sigh. "I better go. I don't want to cause anymore speculation." I push the chair back, drop a kiss on Gramps' lean cheek, and go get ready.

An hour later, I stride through the halls of Rosemont in my nerdy attire. Funny, how things that had seemed earthshakingly important before mean squat now. So what if I'm not popular or a beauty queen? There are a lot worse places to be than Rosemont High. Outside of my school world, there are soulless monstrosities.

I shiver. I'm trying hard not to think of insane scientists, not to remember. The lab cost me my innocence. I've met the monsters in the closets.

I look for Tyler but don't see him.

"Hey, Piper, hope you're feeling better, heard you had the flu." One of Holly's friends calls as I walk into English.

"I am thanks. It was nasty stuff." I keep my voice at the same low pitch I normally use but smile and nod.

I scoot in next to Holly.

"How are you?" She leans toward me.

"I'm fine." I smile.

Class begins. I'm afraid Miss Sweeney might faint when I voluntarily answer a question on Romeo and Juliet. She recovers quickly and smiles her approval.

When the bell rings, several people stop me in the hall and ask how I'm feeling. They drift away as Fahrenbacher swaggers up.

"Hello, Edgar."

"Piper." He dips his chin at me. "Are you feeling better?"

"Yes, I am."

"Want to go out Friday?"

Holly gasps. I poke her in the ribs. "Sorry, I've got plans. Why don't you ask Sophia? I think she likes you." I've seen her throw glances his way.

"Yeah? Maybe, I will." He throws out his chest and saunters away. I watch him disappear down the hall. I'm beginning to think it's my attitude that needs adjustment, not the other kids'. Though I'm afraid Fahrenbacher will always be doing his version of 'kick the dog' with some poor hapless being.

"Boy, when you come out of your shell, you do it in a big way. Now if we could get rid of the shell." Holly throws a disparaging look at my nondescript attire.

"No can do, Hol."

"I understand, hush, hush," she whispers.

Holly may not understand exactly what's going on, but the kidnapping has made her aware how necessary my disguise is.

The day passes quickly. I keep expecting Tyler to talk to me but he keeps his distance.

The next few days are much the same. I'm more comfortable around my classmates. Holly sticks to me like glue while Tyler stays away. It's a puzzle.

Before I know it, the weekend's here. I miss Tyler. My heart aches. As much as I've fought against being with him, now the idea of losing him is unbearable.

I spend a quiet Saturday with Gramps. We both enjoy it. When evening approaches he shoos me out, knowing I'm longing for the water.

As the sun drifts westward, I hurry to the ocean. Instead of diving, I walk down. I want to squish wet sand between my toes, breathe in salty air, and watch the violent crimsons and purples of sunset.

I stand on the edge of the beach. The water plays over my feet, the soft air caresses my skin. I'm free. For a moment, I close my eyes, at peace.

"Piper."

I whirl around. My stomach flutters and my knees grow weak. My insides do a little dance of joy. "Tyler. My hero. I've been wanting a chance to thank you for rescuing me."

I wait for him to come to me, put his arms around me and kiss me till there's no strength left in my body. But he just stands there, fidgeting.

My heart clenches. He doesn't want me anymore. I won't make it difficult for him. I owe him too much. I clear my throat and straighten my shoulders. "What is it?"

"The lab is closed."

"Excuse me?"

"Jackson went back. The lab is closed."

"Closed?" Joel and Amy are gone. My heart tightens. I bite my lip. They're the only two people I know who are like me. The only two that truly understand what I am.

"There's no one there. I'm sorry. I know how much Joel meant to you."

That pulls me off the dark path I'm traveling. I look at him intently. Is this the problem? Joel?

"I've got to believe Joel and Amy are all right." My stomach knots and my heart contracts. "They're too valuable to let anything happen to." It's true. Dr. Stranger will protect them at all costs. Somehow, I will find them again.

"I don't understand." He holds up a hand before I can say anything, "You don't need to explain."

I take a step towards him. "You deserve explanations. It's time and past." I take a deep breath. "Do you still care about me, Tyler?"

"Care is a tepid word for how I feel about you." His eyes spark, go dark. "You've no idea. I care," he emphasizes the word, "enough not to come between you and Joel."

I hold out my hands. Reluctantly, he takes them. I give his warm fingers a small squeeze, trying to make him understand what I'm about to say. "Of course, I care about Joel. Like calls to like. It's a pull that's hard to ignore. But I love you, Tyler. Probably more than is healthy for either of us."

He goes absolutely white before warm color comes surging back. He reaches out, pulls me to him, and kisses me hard, his breath hot on my face, in my mouth. My senses dance at the taste of peppermint on his tongue, the scent of salt on his skin.

Finally, he grasps my shoulders and pushes me away. He continues to hold me up or I'll fall. "I love you so much I could explode with the need of it. I don't understand what you're talking about between you and Joel, but I don't need to, as long as you love me."

I take his hand. "Come into the water with me, there's something I want to show you."

We dive in and splash around like puppies. I go under several times then as the sun goes completely under the water, I chuff.

Tyler stares at me. "What did you just do? I don't understand."

I paddle in the water in front of him. "I'm a mutant. I have dolphin DNA. The lab that captured me…" My voice hitches but I continue, "Was planning on using me to make more little mutants."

"You're a mutant?"

"That's right." I can't get a read on his reaction.

He looks away. Tension builds. A seagull flaps his wings overhead and squawks. The harsh sound accentuates my discomfort. Did I make a mistake telling him?

I must have. He's not saying anything. My throat clogs. It's a good thing we're in the water. The tears welling in my eyes won't be noticeable. I turn toward shore.

His voice stops me. "And Joel is a mutant, too?"

I push air from my lungs and flip around. "Yeah, first generation, not second generation like me. Now you know my deep dark secret. If you've changed your mind about the love thing, I understand." My gaze doesn't meet his. If he rejects me, I'll die. I tap the water with my fingers, making small frothy geysers.

Silence stretches between us, broken only by the occasional slap of a wave and the answering call of another gull. Finally, he says, "So I'll be the only guy at Rosemont whose girlfriend is a mutant?"

I raise my head and catch the laughter in his eyes. "Yeah." I nod. "Looks like."

"I guess it's time my folks get to know you and Mr. Dunn. Maybe we should have that picnic we've been talking about."

Before I can respond, something bumps against my leg. I dive down and come face to face with a dolphin, a dolphin with a scar on her head.

Bubbles explode from my mouth and I throw my arms around her, chattering underwater, "Oh, my little beauty. Joel kept his word. You're free."

The three of us play in the water a long time. Finally, when the gray waves sparkle from the reflection of stars, we head back to shore. The dolphin follows till we hit the shallows then veers off.

Streaming water, Tyler and I wade to the beach. The dolphin brings back memories of the lab. Memories I'd just as soon forget. I take a deep breath. Nothing can happen to me here. I'm home and I'm safe. I have Tyler, Gramps, Holly, friends at Rosemont and somewhere Joel and Amy. Everything's going to be okay. Yeah, I'll have to continue with my nerd disguise but I can live with that. And dealing with Fahrenbacher…well that's pretty small potatoes after being a lab rat.

Echoing my thoughts, Tyler says, "Wait till Holly gets a load of you." He pauses. "Or aren't you going to tell her?"

"Yeah, eventually, but that's as far as it goes. To the rest of the world, I'll still be a geeky nerd."

"From what I've seen this week, the geeky nerd has found her niche at school."

"Appears so." Suddenly, a blurry recollection that I've managed to keep in the back of my brain surfaces. It wasn't a dream. I just wanted to believe it was. My legs give. "Oh my God."

"Piper, what is it?" Tyler pulls me to my feet and wraps his arms around me. "It's okay, baby. Whatever it is, we'll get through it together."

I know he means it. He's proved it. No matter how cataclysmic my problems, he'll stand beside me. And this is cataclysmic, no doubt about it.

Tenderly, he pushes strands of hair away from my face. He tips up my chin. "Can you tell me what's wrong?"

I take a deep breath. "They've got my egg."

His eyes widen; his face registers shock. As I watch, astonishment changes to anger. Resolve firms his boyish features. "We'll just have to get it back, won't we?"

Determination stiffens my spine. Not only will I get my egg back, I owe Dr. Stranger for what he did to my mom. Did he run her off the road and cause her death? I don't know. Maybe I never will, but one thing I do know: I won't be satisfied till I hunt him down and put him out of business.

My life will never be easy, never be without danger. I'm a dolph-girl. But I'm also a survivor. I look at Tyler. I've got too much to live for to do anything else.

A slap against the water causes me to turn. The little dolphin is back. She chatters at me, shoots out of the water, and thumps back in. She reminds me of Joel. For a moment, my heart tightens. How does one deny the call of like-to-like, blood-to-blood? What will happen when I see him again?

Tyler takes my hand and smiles. My heart lightens. I'll cross that bridge when I come to it.

Meet the Author

Multi-published author Sandra Cox writes paranormal YA, YA Fantasy, Paranormal Romance, Time-Travel Romance, Historical Romance, and Metaphysical Nonfiction. She lives in sunny North Carolina with her husband, a brood of critters, and an occasional foster cat. Although shopping is high on the list, her greatest pleasure is sitting on her screened in porch, sipping coffee and enjoying a good book while listening to the birds and other outdoor creatures. She's a vegetarian and has a yellow belt in Muay Thai.

Acknowledgements

Many thanks to:
My editor Paige Christian
Beta readers--Jewel Adams
Mike Cox
Karen Gray (In Remembrance)
Margaret McNeely

www.ingramcontent.com/pod-product-compliance
Lightning Source LLC
Chambersburg PA
CBHW022152260626
47155CB00017B/1844